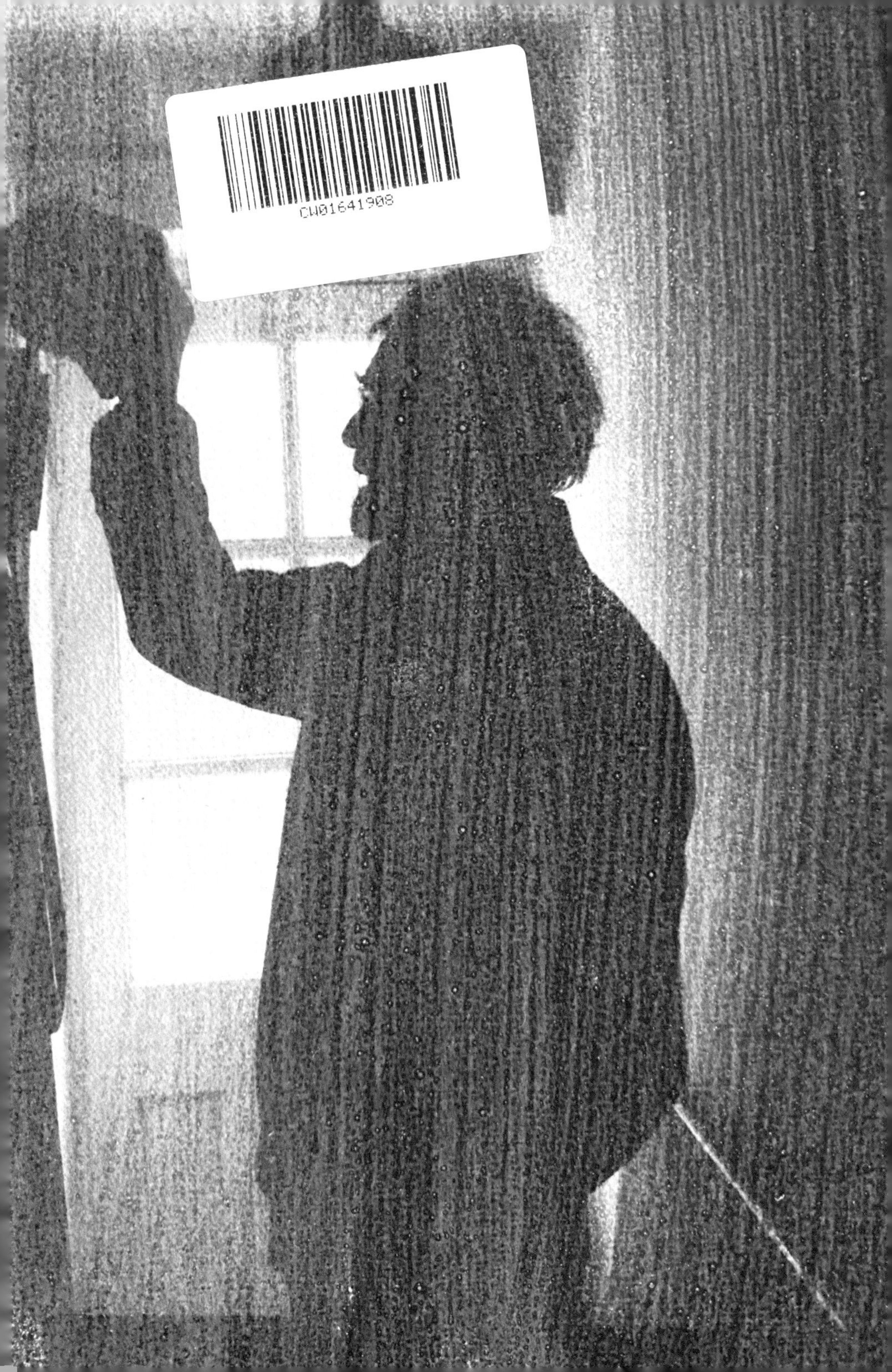

the ART of the MATTER

Claire Steele

Constellations Press

First published in 2026
by Constellations Press

Typeset by Constellations Press
Printed and bound in the UK through Xpedient Book Print

A CIP record for this book is available from the British Library

MIX
Paper | Supporting responsible forestry
FSC® C013604
FSC
www.fsc.org

ISBN 978-1-917000-161

for Duncan –

we were children with scuffed knuckles and rough cheeks,

sent out to play, because play was what everyone should aspire to

Introduction

This memoir is a series of meditations on home and belonging, conducted via the relationship between parent and child. My father was an artist born into a family of miners, and the first member of the family to go to art college or further education of any kind. He grew up in post-war Britain, with a widowed mother and a wicked stepfather. It was a home where there wasn't much time, or love, for either literature or the arts. Indeed, they were considered both wasteful and effeminate. Dad died in 2018, when I was running a writing retreat in Morocco. I got the news the morning that we arrived. I have never resented my work; I have been fortunate all my life to love what I do, but that week I had to screw up every bit of willpower to stay with the words, and be curious about what they would reveal. One of the greatest lessons of my childhood was to make a creative space and to step into it. This has proved again and again to be my salvation, guiding me through grief, desolation and two years in solitude during 2020/21, living in a single room, unable to see family or friends.

I have found his death almost impossible to contemplate or to believe in. There must be some flaw in my makeup that resists a belief in the blindingly obvious. This memoir began as a series of a hundred words a day, considering what it has been like to be fathered by an artist – this man: my father – and to have lived a life that has been informed from its earliest conversations by a deep, creative attention to the world. One of the profoundest losses has been the collective value of those insights that he brought to us, and now I am discovering them again, or different ones, through my regard of his work.

I understand memoir to be the kind of writing that does not simply attend to what happened, but to how what happened changed us. It strikes me that this is also the transformative work of art. It's not the image itself that is important – it's how that image changes the way we understand the world and ourselves. This book is a kind of self-portrait with my dad, and a way of extending the relationship and keeping it alive. Art is where we can meet a version of ourselves with all the surprise and delight of meeting a stranger. It moves us to another place, and we need a whole new language to describe it.

Claire Steele
January 2026

Father's Day 2022. On which, an idea makes itself known to me about what it is I should be doing. I don't know why I didn't think of it before. But here I am, on a day you wouldn't have cared to have acknowledged, beginning to make my way towards you. It has been a very textured, grooved and layered day. The fields are being cut for hay, marked with lines and circles, the way an artist marks things. The evening provides a silver line scored between the clouds and the land. Throughout my life, you taught me to look again. *Look again*, which I do, but nothing that I see coalesces, exactly. There are shifting shadows. My eyes ache with lights which I perceive but do not quite see. If I look for them, they vanish. On my desk there is a photograph of you in silhouette, printed onto a piece of glass. You are a blurred, grey shape, lifting a hat, almost as if you were composed of soot or iron filings. The surface that holds you, on which you seem to tremble, looks solid, but I know it isn't. Everything is constantly shifting.

Be a good workman first, you say. It will never prevent you from being a genius.

When I pay attention, the world rewards that. There is not a single thing that does not flourish under attention. I let my mind focus on you and things fall into my lap. Or into my laptop. Either way, it feels like these are the ways in which we connect now. A small silver head you wore on a chain, which we thought long gone, was in an old medicine bottle, marked 'head', along with some teeth: a bit grim, perhaps, but precious. As I shake them into my palm, I recall the skeleton of the cat that you dug up from the garden at Pear Tree Cottage, with Mum's chewed-up wedding ring hidden in the soil of its belly. I have thought about this, and I decided it would not be right to call the remains feline. I think feline requires a body. And now neither the cat nor you have that. Other treasures that have travelled from one world to the next: scraps of paper with cryptic notes in your handwriting; a navigator's compass; a snatch of film of a room, where you must have been just out of shot, and your voice saying: 'you are lucky'. It made me cry, but I could not stop playing it.

Now and then, I go to stand next to your bench, and I find it preoccupied with you, by which I mean you had occupied its space so many times it was enough for me just to stand there, next to the bench, and miss you; to feel myself on the brink of tears, which happens both in the eyes and the throat. When I have had enough, by which I mean as much as I can bear, for it is never really enough, I head back out into the empty space between the barn, the house and the woods where the rooks are calling and the sky hurtles overhead, chasing my emotions right out of me.

It's a different feeling standing in the barn – with your bench, and all your tools – from being in the presence of a painting. I am a child in the company of your bench, consoled by its scale, its humble willingness to press itself to whatever task there might be. I think it will take me a lifetime with a painting to finish the conversations we can have there, about the world, going on forever.

Just as if I asked for a sign, the post brought a card, with a photograph of you from 1974 in it, your gaze grey and clear. In 1974 you were still painting. You hadn't given it up yet for the kiln. When I think of it now, I wonder if you gave it up as a matter of scale. When we lived at The Gables, it seemed obvious that the house was more studio than home. It was a mansion of freezing Victorian rooms, full of northern light. When we moved to King's Head, the seventeenth-century ceilings were low, the rooms were small. Your notion of the world was vast. All those big canvases. Did they get stashed in the barn? You turned to fire. Melting colour to glass, etching into metal. What was your subject matter? Icarus. Daedalus. Fathers and sons. Sons and suns. I squint as I try to see all the way back there, where the light bleaches everything out and time was a makeshift scaffold on which to hang the sun.

What does it mean to be doing this work? Resurrecting the dead? Wouldn't it be better to go and see to the dinner? Attend to the needs of the mortals? I think of the times I wish now that I'd spent with you, being really present, really listening, and I think I should be doing that with them. I shouldn't defer that, make the same mistake again. Nevertheless, here I am.

In the direction of belongings, you were always indulgent, giving yours away, encouraging us to get the best we could afford, even if it meant pinching somewhere else. We never bought on tick, never had a credit card, never coveted more than the world might provide. When you were thirty, you gave your only coat to an old man – or perhaps he wasn't old, but just badly used – shivering in a shop doorway, and it was two years before you could buy another. The sparrows squabbled in the puddles of cracked ice and you walked back in your shirt sleeves, coming home to your numberless obligations. We hardly see sparrows these days. The little birds that were a ubiquitous part of my childhood are all but invisible now.

Driving through the hills of the north, from Skipton across the A629 to Silsden, the late sun was like a molten copper penny. Behind that, you said, is starlight, but as my gaze flickered fast as the landscape seen through the car window, it seemed hardly credible. Years later, I would sit in a lecture theatre and be told how there is a tribe that asserts the sun is a white cockatoo, and that that is not a metaphor but an observation, much like we might say a man is six foot two. I think of other ways we could describe the sun: the sun is a white stone, steady in the grey wall of the wind; a sprinkling of sequins roughly spelling the word shine on the surface of the canal; feathers falling; a son, falling through fire and air into the sea. The sun coming out of the cloud is you throwing your head back and clapping your hands in laughter.

This garden is so full of time it holds me in its breath. There is a lot to be done. I walk around it and think of the wonderful gardens you created: the night-scented stocks of summer breezing in through the kitchen window; the green rooms we could pass through to find some new delight. Then there came a moment when you thought it might be right to cement a tree into the ground, to protect it from the storms, and that was when we knew for sure that dementia had eaten into what you could be certain of. Now, I have your Solomon's Seal, your gooseberry bush, your wallflowers. They are doing well. All these plants with their roots in the past and their fruit or petals, just as powerfully reminiscent of another era as if they had been pressed between the pages of a book or in a Victorian flower press. All the plants we have discovered together: speedwell, betony, birds-foot trefoil. The hedgerows were a riot of cranesbill and dog-daisies. We walked the moors and found spotted wild orchids. Listen to that, you said, as we shared an apple. The buzzard circling overhead tipped her wing ever so slightly. The sheep bleated my piteous name.

Unless I get myself up onto Lines Hill, which is, unsurprisingly, one of my favourite roads in the Vale of Aylesbury, the skies here are never quite big, not like at home. Here the skies struggle to lift themselves above the noise. They are often best seen reflected in the water. Where I live now, you can see the whole sky dropped into a reservoir, or a stream, or a puddle; the wet and broken roads cradling small saucers of sky.

Into this thought slides the memory of a day of rain and tears, and childish fingers burned to blisters on the oven ring. I was three, or maybe four, and I'd been told not to touch, but my fingers were drawn to the bright orange circle on the top of Auntie Florrie's electric oven. I don't think I was wilfully being disobedient. Perhaps I simply couldn't imagine that what I was being told not to touch was that beautiful glowing thing, which pulled me towards it. There are times now, when I look at a painting and I see the echo of that ring. It might burn still, but I cannot tear myself away from it. I must have been standing on a chair, helping. As soon as I was delivered back into your arms, we walked up past the tannery into the woods, walking fast, fast as grown-ups, anything to move me away from what had occurred (you know, I still do that).

You encouraged me to look up and see what shapes the rain made in the sky as it fell. The sky at the abattoir that day was also reflected in the road's craters, but oil-slicked and blood-slicked into rainbows, as though the ground was seething, as though it, too, was burning at its extremities. The rain reformed itself endlessly. Behind us the thunder rumbled, or perhaps that was just the cows, panicking.

Things we collected from the roads:

Iron lace, rusted and flattened into filigree by traffic and weather
Dead frogs x 3, in various attitudes of trying to outjump a car
Broken eggs from robins, blackbirds; occasionally, a thrush
Coins, if there were any

Once, in London, a wallet full of twenties, which you took to the police station; they looked at you as though you were mad, or had forgotten how people normally behave. Their expressions, puzzled and pitying, were a foretaste of how people would adjust their reactions to you years later, when your wits were misplaced by dementia.

Things we collected from the fields:

Sheep skulls x 3
The jawbone of a hare
A badger pelt which you cured (which did not mean made better)
Feathers, lots of them, often from corvids
Iron age flints
Stones with holes in them, stones with fossils in them, seedheads
Sheep wool snagged on barbed wire, unravelling

Things we collected from the rivers:

More iron lace, bent out of shape, flaking into water
Marbles, knocked and scuffed, jam jars of sticklebacks
Rusted tins
Driftwood
Bones
Stones

Some of these things occasionally made their way into your paintings. When I enter the studio now, the things that remain on the shelves and sills and ledges seem to make invisible adjustments, as though they can tell I am not you, but as though they are pleased to share the space with me anyway.

So, I rummage about in this world made up of all these beautiful and sorry materials, collating and repurposing them. Wherever you are, walk perceptively, you told me; pay attention. There were swifts in the sky today, and small pears on the tree. In other news, they have released wild bison, once thought extinct, into Kent; and made the strongest telescope ever conceived, so that we can see stars that existed at the beginning of the universe. The past tumbles down to us in dust and stones and ferns and fruit, and even in the air that we breathe. We see things now we couldn't see before. Honestly, I am looking for you everywhere.

If memory is olfactory, here are the smells I remember you by: the sweet smell of petrol being pumped into the tank of our maroon Renault 4; pipe tobacco and bitter dottle; home brew and the maltings as we drive through Leeds. It's a shining, golden smell, inciting pleasure with a little shiver in it. It's known as the soul of the beer, you tell me. It comes from barley. The light is thinning through the petrol haze on the road; a vision dithers and then it's gone. The next road we drive down, we are in rain, a sudden storm. A sky the black of wet slate roof-tiles. As you drive I watch the rain scintillating the windscreen, dazzling it. One wiper is behind the beat, knocking a lament against the glass, leaving a ghost of water behind it.

By the time we reach the hills, we are back in the brilliance, the restless splendour of the light as it moves over the land. You tell me about the barley, how it is steeped, like tea, then husked and sprouted, and then withered, which means steamed. It's not the right word then, I protest. And while the sun rests its chin on the land, we seek the word that would give some truth to the alchemy that releases the soul of the beer. Kilning, you say. And I agree.

Every so often, I go up into the studio and spend time with the unfinished paintings. Each time I see them, I understand something more entire than the last time. To begin with, all I could see was the heart-wrench of the unfinished work. The underthought, as it were. The relationship between what might have been there and what now could never be.

Then I began to see something else forming, almost shyly. A kind of everlastingness. The flattened paint tube, reversed. A misshapen rusted circle of rescued metal. Something came to rest on the canvas, like a sky might come to rest upon the surface of a lake. The sort of arrival that if you looked straight at it, you couldn't see. The sort of arrival that is so fleeting it might never have occurred. Now, when I stand in front of the unfinished works, I see that what is before me is the mystery.

I begin with an idea, and then it becomes something else. Picasso said that, you told me. He also said some people turn the sun into a yellow spot and some people turn a yellow spot into the sun. I am thinking about all the different ways you painted the sun: a black sun edged in muted turquoise – the colour of the light lifting off Semerwater as the day drops; a rough gold disc cut from a paint tube; a broken red line; cement mixed with copper and gamboge, rosso Veneto, raw umber. Winter suns low in winter skies. Sometimes we can only see the thing we are looking at when we see it reversed, in reflection; the way, in fact, we always see ourselves. Tonight, the sun dropped behind the great hill up to Burtersett, and the lake lost its light. The grebes and the moorhens arranged themselves as if for a nineteenth-century watercolour. The hillside stooped to meet its own shadow on the surface of the water, then strengthened into its massive silhouette.

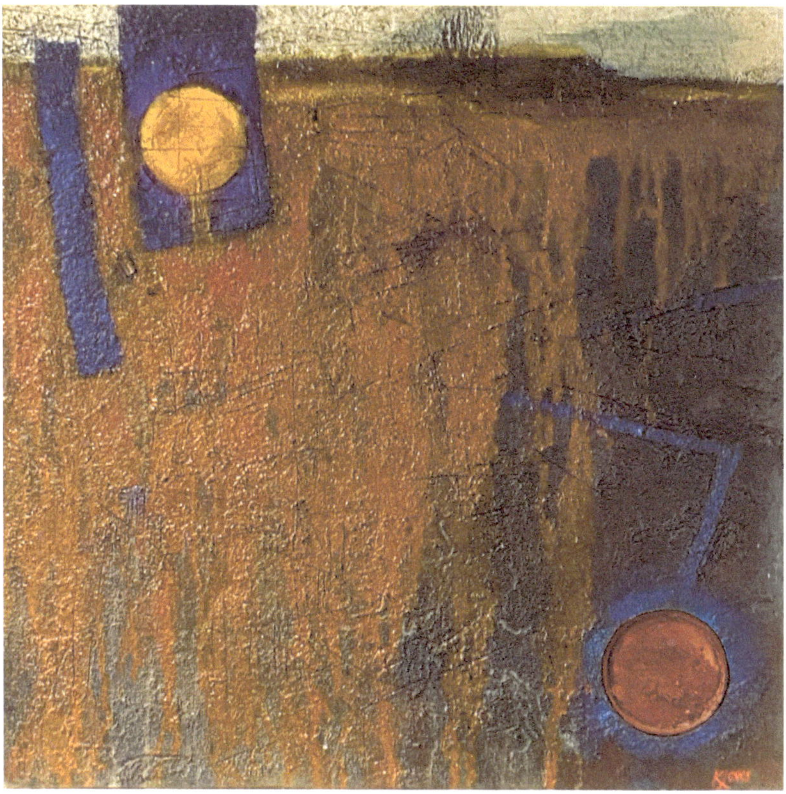

Trouble in mind: the smell of Nag Champa rising on the air; you playing the guitar with the broken neck, mended with the escutcheon of silver that you cut and hammered yourself. Or perhaps it was some other silver-coloured metal. *I'm blue*: the wind is shaking the rhododendrons into the ground, rain staining the petals tea-coloured. You were blue for much of our childhood. Not blue, so much as the colour of a beetle's back when you turn over a spade of soil. Not blue, so much as black. What does it mean to be blue? Beyond the love of God. In Morocco, the blue tribe, the Tuareg, were so called because they were not Muslim; they were infidels, wanderers in the desert. Even Jesus went there.

You were so blue you were beyond the love of family. As a child I was sent in to you to ask you if you loved us: Go in, Mum said, giving me a little push. Go and ask Daddy if he still loves us. I crossed the vast desert of the faithless space to ask you. You raised your head, but your blue-grey eyes were dark. You had no words to bring you out of the fathomless blue that hung as heavy as the North Sea above you. Under the blue, as underpainting, was the rage. Terrifying bursts of furniture-destroying, wall-scarring fury.

But I won't be blue always. Who could have foreseen how true that would become? Who could have predicted that in the decades to come, dementia would make you forget your blues? If I'd had to hazard a guess, I'd have said that you'd have raged against the erosion of your mind, that wild, unique, particular thing with which you revealed – or maybe created – the world for us. But instead, you became so mellow. Gentle. You'd never known such beautiful weather. Never had a cross word.

There were times when your dementia embarrassed me, when you said things that shredded the social fabric and left us scrabbling for a bit of something to make us decent again. Now, I would give anything to be caught like that by you, willing to defend every one of your indiscretions in order to be present again with you.

Imagine if the world had no blue in it. The ancient Greeks had no word for blue; their seas were wine-dark. In Italy, the Virgin's clothes were pink until Simone Martini brought back the colour of heaven.

That big old sun is gonna shine on my back door some day. I open the front door to Pear Tree Cottage, the one that exists only in my mind, or in photographs. There you are, rocking in the chair, singing to your old guitar. I'm always doing things I can't do, you say; that's how I get to do them. Then you wink at me and make one of your arms longer than the other. Picasso said that. Of course he did.

In this narrow room, which houses my books and your paintings, the sun momentarily throws a veil of light – which has the opacity of a sucked orange fruit gum – across the wall, transforming your work and my books, and then turning down the intensity, degree by degree, until the world is as it was, only greyer.

Things that made you rage: three teaspoonfuls of salt mistakenly sweetening your tea; the work not working; poor workmanship; your stepfather; stupidity; a bag of sugar caught in the flex of an electric iron, losing its precarious balance in the crammed car as we motored to Wales, and hitting you on the back of the head when you were forced to brake suddenly; taking an iron on a camping holiday; incompetent map-reading; incompetence in general.

In the wet churchyard, I navigate the rough hillside path down to the graves, a gradient so steep that I am both physically and emotionally on a tilt. The evidence is incontrovertible that everyone dies, but I still can't make that feel true for you. I have a steadfast resistance to that in my heart.

A small brown moth shivers on a tilting headstone. Margaret Iveson, who fell asleep on the 11th of October (the year is obscured), has a trio of rosettes of gold lichen on her stone. The graveyard is crammed with people of whom nothing remains except the imprint of love and loss in the air around their graves, and their names and dates, and sometimes even those are so weathered that they are eroding into not-being. Some of them must have been important, but the weather has resolved them. All that remains is the certainty that their name began with V, or it had a V in it. Rain slants across the field. The grave above yours, in this graveyard on the slope, belongs to Jean Poole. That would have made you laugh, her genes trickling down into yours.

On West Cliff beach we gathered filigree seaweeds, stones and gull feathers. The rocks were skirted with bleached driftwood, piles of seabones thrown against the land. The seaside was the place for big blues, and hurling oneself at the rope, whatever that meant. You had the core of an apple in your pocket for the donkeys.

Usually you ate your apples whole, core and all, even the gowky bits that stuck in my throat when I tried to be like you. I can still feel the soft lips of the donkeys moving in the palm of my hand, trying to muzzle up the apple, and the scour of their coarse, sandy coats against my bare legs. Later, from the unzipped bedroom wall of the tent, we watched as the moon stretched the sky into the black shades of scorched aluminium. Shadows returning. There were all those days of remembering, never imagining that the big forgetting was heading our way.

Tree-stain on a child's bridesmaid's dress. A three-year-old disappears when it is time to take the wedding photos. Everything always needs our full attention. A different wedding, a different bridesmaid's dress, and a white bonnet covered in sugar-stiffened voile daisies, each with its yellow centre. A different wedding, a child in a crimplene A-line dress, long white socks and white patent leather shoes. In all of these wedding memories, one of your children is scowling and the other is going round the tables, finishing off the glasses of sweet sherry. I cannot imagine where you were in any of these.

Being with the dead requires attention. I think of you lying there in the Aysgarth graveyard, and wonder what might be distracting you. What is making itself known down there? Are worms and beetles making their marks, gnawing precise tunnels under the cardboard box? I comb the landscape for words, trying to recognise what I need to pay attention to. I keep coming back to your name chiselled into stone. It's not bad, but I think you'd have made a better job of it yourself.

All light needs its opposite in order to exist. When I look at your paintings now, I see how cleverly you see the light: how it moves against the dark, how it vibrates, like someone has struck a tuning fork. In the bottom right-hand corner of this large and complex painting is a quiet lozenge of yellow, softened by grey. It is the light caught inside a buttercup on a day that will soon turn to rain. Who else but you would have had the tact to make that a stripe? There it is at the bottom of the painting, unfinished business, a scuff of gold. A conversation still being conducted through the marks you made, the work you did, the work you were. You didn't always sign your work, but it holds your identity, nevertheless.

I wonder how much any of us leaves behind. The day feels as hot as the summer of '76 when I lay day after day on the grass at King's Head, just listening to the earth's small sounds: beetles moving through the blades, leaves shifting, the heat crackling all around me. All day I would lie there, in the weeks of revising for my exams, waiting for the evening to fall and the scent of the night-scented stocks to rise in the dusk. Nothing of us lives there now, not even the negative of us, somehow imprinted into the earth. Nothing, except perhaps the stocks, still perfuming the breeze with all the sweetness you could muster.

To be of use ought to be the aim of our lives, you tell me. The barn is full of meticulously collated, useful things, each casting their shadow. Screws, nails, brackets, sprockets. Three hundred miles away: metal, a handful of soil from the land I still call home. How do we speak this language from some childhood time we might have lost? Gradely; now frame yourself. As in: look lively.

More real than ever, more exact than remembering, the light comes in through the small cobwebby window, picks out the copper dust upon the surface of the bench. Dust, lighter than air, casting no shadow. Or maybe not dust, maybe just the smudge of all your ghost selves, handling the things that made you useful.

Recalling the beauty of alphabet under your hand, each letter making a perfect shape, I remember you patiently showing me how to write and how to read. I remember this as patient, although I know that wasn't the case with Duncan. You gave me the word yellow, written in raw cobalt-yellow ink, upon a piece of white card and placed upon a dark green wall. The upper-case O, you said, is never a circle. Always the interior shape should be an ellipsis, shaped like an olive. Ellipsis, Greek for falling short. These formed my earliest memories of written words, not just the beauty of them in the mouth but the beauty of them on the wall.

I learned recently that our alphabet was devised by people who could not read. I had thought the word came from the Greek (*alpha* and *beta*), but I have just discovered that in remotest Sinai there are inscriptions that show the hieroglyph for an ox: *aleph* and that for a house: *bet*, and that these were the words that gave us the alphabet, the signs on the walls, that we use today. Between yellow olive and wild olive, a house, and beside the house an ox, slowly ruminating on the colours of yellow and ochre, and what the ratio might be between the inside of the letter and the outside.

The light opens up a shadow window on the wall and quivers there. It feels like the visual equivalent of a prayer, a bet with the unknown. From time to time, I feel your presence rather than your absence, a mostly unacknowledged blessing.

This shaking light, composed of both inside and outside, makes me think of how intimate, how close, the unknown is, like the (absent) sound between two sounds. I wonder if that is what it was like when things that had been known blended into the unknown for you. Not the thing itself, but the image of the thing, fleeting. Shadows on the cave wall. The sun moves, the window shuts. A cloud has shifted the wall into repose.

A ghost casts no shadow, you said, but I don't know what to make of that.

I became half a memory for you, not quite myself, not quite anyone else, though blurring into other people (usually Mum) sometimes. I became the image of an image, blotched and bleached with age – smiling out of an old photo of someone who looked like me once. It takes light to make a photograph. The shape of an image on a surface. At Amulet, the shop we had in Silsden, you developed photographs upstairs in a home-made darkroom. We would see a thing coming into being. Sometimes we would see it failing to come into being, floating off the paper and vanishing into a chemical solution. How does it do that? I asked. Now I am thinking how apt a metaphor it is for the mind. How does the mind steady a memory, or just miss it, sink beneath it while the memory hovers tantalisingly above the steadying principle and then vanishes?

Perhaps, in dementia, the image lifts off the memory and floats just beyond recognition. Perhaps, for you, everything that could be forgotten had to find itself echoed in some sort of symmetry, a thing that happened in the past, but was no longer retrievable.

Look at that big cloud. What does it do?

It carries rain, Dad, to the places that need it.

Yes, it does that, but it does something else as well. Does it keep the earth's light in?

What is the word for that thing I've got that I can't remember? You asked. Is it Delilah? The mind judders through hazy metaphors, where one word will substitute for another, where all words are created equal although all are equally obscure. A translator has scrambled the vocabularies of one kind of knowledge for another. Thus, sultry becomes a word for lamplight. Entire pauses allow meaning to drain through, sparkle and then vanish.

As far as I know, people in every nation sing.

Is the word for that voluble?

Whole vistas of people mouth the words as a kind of music rises between us.

Outside, bitter green apples are beginning to form in the old tree. The shadow of a woman fills the empty square of the window. Everything is conveyed doubled, complex as a code. Still, happiness can be found in a bag of jelly babies. Delilah, your room awaits, the double doors are open. Is the word for that wife?

When you are in spontaneous communication with the paint, it is the most magnificent conversation: instinctive, expansive and full of flex. The world appears under the brush, just as Blake knew it, infinite in every mark. I think of Blake's engravings – his hand on the chisel, the idea of work as a means of making the unknown known. Above the workshop, the studio. The tools are different here. Cans of paintbrushes, old toothbrushes, palette knives, rags. The continual discourse between the world and the work still in progress. There are all the familiar references and then there are the places where they move into revelation. One of the greatest gifts of art, and love, you tell me, is that it introduces you to yourself in a way that you could never have otherwise found yourself.

I move the paintings around in the house, just to look again at them and see them in a new light. As I have them in my arms (for these are big pieces), I think of what it means to be alive, to have a life. I think it means to be involved in or attentive to the work of transformation. And, in that sense, all life is art. Or is that a meaningless thing to say?

When I hear the news on the radio, there are times when I am glad you don't have to hear it. What happens when governments are so overblown with their own righteousness that they use the vocabularies of genocide as a matter of course? What happens when we are living in the era of post-truth, and any dissenting voices are thrown into prison? Plato knew that to control society, you should lock up its artists. The artist makes a space that means it is possible to think differently.

You always said art should not have a manifesto. How do we hold that particular conversation now?

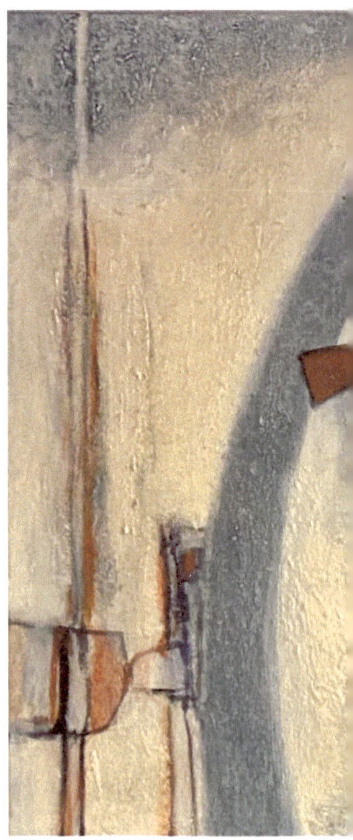

I was asked today what the difference is between a wish and a hope. There is a distinction, though I struggled to formulate it. A hope, I ventured, is articulated in the belief that a thing could happen; a wish is made in the belief that it probably never will. I was thinking about you and our lost conversations.

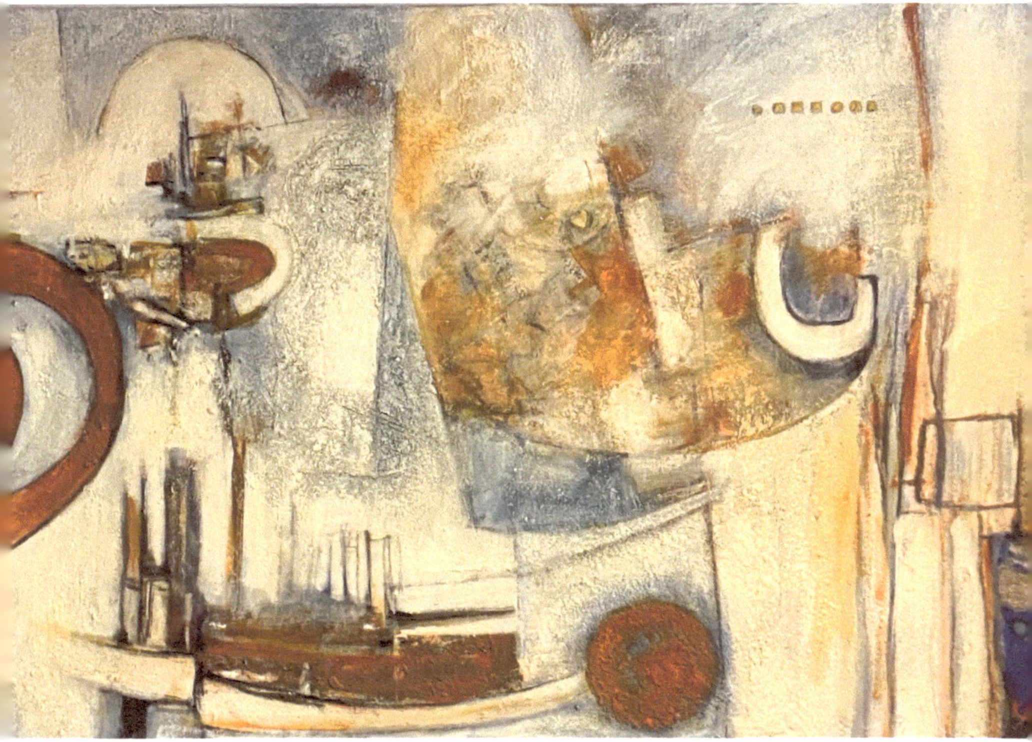

The landscape is a state of mind, you said. It changes quickly.

From Stalling Busk up the stake road across the moors that connect Wensleydale with Upper Wharfedale, the going is rough. Buzzards, if we are lucky, circle overhead. Skylarks, curlews, almost certainly. A gate in the wall at right angles to the path leads us down over waterlogged peat beneath streaming skies. What do we talk about? The white painting. You are pursuing the idea that it might be possible to explore white through white alone. The sky is yellow-white, oily, like the whites of the eyes of someone who has lived a hard life. Flecks of white in the limestone, glinty. Sheep, hardly white. If you hold this up against them – you said, pulling out your A6 sketchbook and turning to a blank page – they almost look black. You know, you said, turning to me, I haven't had depression in the longest while. And, shame on me – because I was struggling and maybe you knew it – I thought: bully for you.

The offside of the dale, seen from the window of your cottage, is a grudging pact between sky and land, shifting for each other according to the light. Sometimes when I look, I cannot tell whether it is the sky streaming or the land. It is dizzying the way this landscape moves around me. It makes my eyes water, reminds me how mortal I am. The landscape is burnt sienna, raw umber, alizarin crimson, painting wet into wet. I found a metal sun for you, full of glitter, points of light beaten into it. It's on the windowsill, next to the crow's skull and the branch from the twisted hazel.

It has been one of those days. Thunder gathers in the clouds in blooms of gold, lead and zinc, and the sky is full of moody fire. Wherever you are, it's not here, and I am stumbling around trying to regain my balance. The day has been a kiln, transfiguring us all. Something dreadful and arresting has me in its grip, like a struck deer on a back road caught in the car's headlights, red pouring from it; like a damaged red admiral butterfly, moving in circles on the stone flag. If you look for signs you will find them. God claps his hands, just as you did, and the sound is absolute. What was it like to die? Were you sucked out of all you knew? Was it just your body, engaged in the last act of forgetting itself? Did you feel yourself getting very small? So small you could hardly be seen with the naked eye? Is that how angels dance on the head of a needle? That precise outline of who you were. Vanishing again and again.

Some things you might spend your time with: a chipped Cowdy glass, a piece of millstone grit with mica in it, broken coffee machines, sludgy with old coffee. The sky is grey as tuna tins, lying low on the hills; daffodils blow in the wind. We pick up whatever we can. We especially pick up small things, things tucked into the crevices and the surfaces of the world. Bits of metal, bits of leaf skeleton. The contexts in which you confuse them grow larger. A wet leaf blown straight from the falls might be a hummingbird for the tenderness with which you handle it. An empty frame against the studio wall percolates the lifelong idea of the work, as once again you sort your collection of chisels into an arrangement that prompts not sadness exactly, but something more oblique than that.

There's a whole vocabulary that is home for me, that no-one around me uses now. 'Lass', for example. And 'our lad'. And he is our lad, he's still our lad. He always will be. When I talk to our lad about you, I still refer to you as 'my dad' even though you are his dad too. And now I am mindful of these fierce possessives, articulating how we belong to each other. Later, there is the vocabulary of landscapes: becks and ginnels, capsteps, and I see us there still laikin' and, to tell the truth, I'm capped. Behind this, there are mines of men in the dark. Maybe they are mouthing to each other the words that two generations later we have all but forgotten, flickerings of sound in the black tunnels, making themselves understood.

A blue tit bounced out of the ivy and onto the old Victorian fireplace I have in the garden. It eyed me, its marvellous bluetittery vibrating in the momentary light between us. Then it opened its stripy wings, flew onto the buddleia and was gone. You taught me so much about the birds, their calls, their feathers, their songs. Now there is only a void in my memory, edged with concentration, and every so often, phrases of delight and alarm. I don't forget, but also, I don't remember very well.

Imagine if everything we remembered still existed in some endless way. There I am as a child, picking up a handful of stones from the sunshiney earth, arranging them; there I am gathering watercress under Kilnsey Crag; learning to drive; getting drunk. Do the memories have to have a person in them to persist? What about the green fringing on the velvet tablecloth in Central Avenue; the smell of pipe tobacco and turps, and old spice; the sound of a man's heart under the weight of a dozing daughter. If the stones were different, the memories would be someone else's.

The hammer beats a flat square of metal into a curve. When this is achieved, anything and everything else will work. A handful of copper dust. Death steps aside, leaving a small scratch, just a mark to let us know he was passing. The things of this world are here somewhere. From the back of the ivy, the blue tit's reason for being. Delight, Dad, pure delight.

Everything we have arises from what became of you: these images, these tools, these words. We are made of dust and we return to dust. No doubt there is still some the precious dust of you in the world you inhabited, your fingerprints on everything, but vanishing now. I missed the last sound you made. Then I missed the space between that sound and the unending silence and the realisation that of all the things I would ever hear for the rest of my life I would never hear your voice again, or at least, not with your breath behind it. The voice, which is so unique it is impossible to commit it to memory, to learn it by heart. I am reaching for everything that once seemed so normal, wanting to experience it again and marvel at it.

Things that move fast: moods, ideas; expressions; you – on the bogeycart you made for your grandchildren, hurtling down the steep hill that curved from the skyline down to Busk House and then beyond to the lake, whipping round the bends towards the church and the rough patch of ground you must have hoped would provide a natural brake. One hand on the ropes, one high in the air as you whooped past us in a blur. Things that move fast: a single incident that serves as metonymy for a whole life.

I am prompted to think about inheritance: what we leave of the self to others, what you left of your paintings, the multiple expressions of a single idea. On the doorway to the hotel where I am staying is a sign; it reads: don't forget the art. They have done studies now that demonstrate that looking at art, really engaging with it, is as good for a person's health as exercise. You bequeathed me a lifetime of looking again, an understanding of the comedy of adversity, and an insight into the battle against the huge imprecision of forgetfulness. I consider the demolished image of myself in the city fountain and wonder if there is something to be seen there, and if that was what Hockney was looking for in his inventions of reversed perspective, showing the space expanding away rather than diminishing. Isn't that as close to heaven as we might come?

Because you forgot so much, I am trying to remember everything. Most of all, I try to remember the things you told me. For example, what you said as you handed me the jawbone of a sheep: you don't have to know what something has been, in order to hold it.

How long is long? Never long enough: the length of a night, the length of a life. Too long: the length of time it takes to miss someone when you know you will never see them again. Does an artist really die? The work is still here – prompting new thoughts, new ways of seeing. There is a wren on the rooftiles – dipping in and out of the gutter. Everything here is still very busy.

Should I continue? I learned about your death in this weather. The light was shining on the scrub of forest in a land two thousand, one hundred and forty-seven miles from where you were. It wasn't the death I was expecting. Expecting is the wrong word. I wondered what else I had seen and not noticed. The moment felt oddly premature, fragile, as though it needed care. The cry I heard was my own, and the unique sound of you had stopped, somewhere else, quite suddenly. After that, many different kinds of silence, some provisional, some absolute.

A day of knowledge pushing against my resistance. I wonder how many other people died that day, and how many times a soul was shaken from its body into the capacious heavens. Imagine if there were a museum containing one thing from everyone who had died that day. In Zagreb, there is the Museum of Broken Relationships. People donate an object that represents either the break-up or the relationship. There is an axe that someone took to break up every piece of furniture that they owned. There are letters. There are gathered together all the things that seem irrevocably transfigured by loss.

When a person dies, the things they leave behind, in the broken space that once held them, are both pitiful and overwhelming. What remains is the way in which these objects represent remembrance. Everything reminds me of you, but it also only reminds me how much we have lost.

I think of your immense competence when it came to things like houses and how to fettle all the things that might require a mending hand: a roof falling in; a window to be cut into a stone wall; a floor to be laid; a door to be hung. A door leading to all the doors of all the houses we lived in and all those we never lived in. I hope your passing through was easy. Here is the door to everything that is finished and everything that is about to begin, you say, as you hold it open.

I went with Gabriel to see Punchdrunk – *The Burnt City* – and entered a place where violence was unavoidable, but no-one dies. Fear and anger stirred the hot air and we tried to make sense of them, as we moved through the shady scenarios of a vanished, yet terrifyingly present, regime. Perhaps this is as good a metaphor as any for dementia. It was an evening marked by magic, two halves of a shape finding each other in the dark. We walked in a place where we had no history, our history being buried underground with the miners whose history made us. It was the same for everyone in the dark, behind the mask. Two halves of a shape: a man's hands making a coin disappear. This could be Mycenae, or a Northern mill town, or the outer edge of London. When it comes to work, or magic, you tell me (which might also be art): practice doesn't make perfect, it makes improvement.

Twelve questions about art:

What is a work of art?
How can we possibly tell?
Where do our convictions come from?
Is a pocket full of rusted nails art?
Is it the relationship between land and dream as depicted in three lines?
Is it where absolutely nothing becomes absolutely created?
Is it inextricably linked to the ideas of strength or beauty or excellence?
Is it a windowpane obscured by grime?
Is it a disc of ice lifted from a metal bucket?
Is it a pure note sung at the top of a ploughed field?
Is it a matter of God?
Is it a matter of survival?

The distance between you and your art is immeasurable. Your paintings remain mysterious to me. Mysterious and deeply familiar.

Some days, time ruffles. Past and future meet each other coming back, or going forwards. Your fine collection of left-handed gloves was noted, and the dearth of right-handed gloves lamented. Not to worry; we made do with the vagaries of what remains of you. Better than that, you, large as life, clapping your hands together. Self-portrait as a series of single gloves. There were plenty of things from the day that you'd have loved: trestle tables full of hammers and chisels; a wine-rack stacked with rolling pins; a cuckoo clock and the strength it takes to keep sorrow at bay.

Will the circle be unbroken? I am very belatedly moved by how many circles, broken and unbroken, appear in your work.

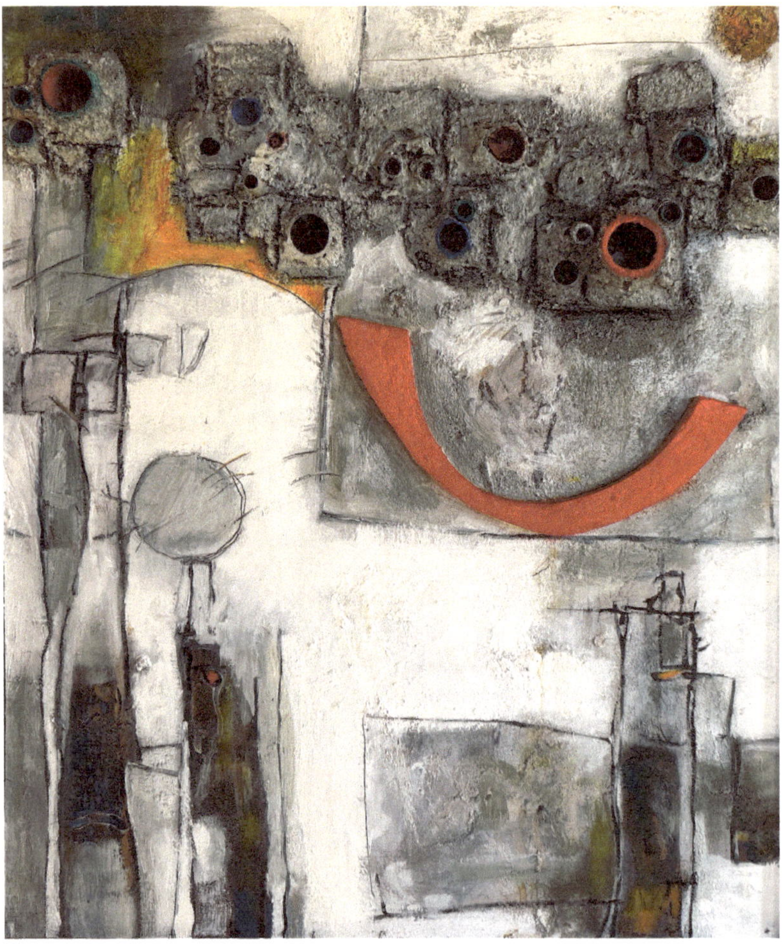

Another day of magical recurrences. There is life in a stone. You can feel that a stone has experienced many things. A copper bowl contains the memory of time and a beating. Today, among the stones and copper bowls, we find a Victorian stick-puppet of Mr Punch, dressed in pink and black silk. The pink silk is almost threadbare now. The pink silk takes us to the very edge of collapse, which is a very beautiful place to arrive. This antique piece of theatre provokes responses that take me right back into childhood. People also leave presence in a place even when they are no longer there, you tell me. We could no more leave Mr Punch behind, than we can leave you behind, than a stone can leave time behind.

Paint, dust, cement, string: all the inscrutable surfaces of a painting nudging each other into a conversation between the real and the symbolic. Marks scored into the surface, potentially something to do with suffering, something to do with plenitude. Perhaps the conversation is a religious one. To do with faith. Perhaps it is romantic. Mr Punch leans over the edge of the pop-up theatre box, demonstrating the body's precarious relationship with the spaces it must inhabit.

Look at how art transforms the basest of materials, you tell me. Then look at how a wall might do the same thing. How lucky we are just to be alive.

That's the way to do it.

In a book of maps, I discovered a set of instructions in your handwriting. No doubt we blundered along. We would not be going there, anyway. It wasn't that we were lost, exactly. Now we have outlived all those places. Towards Whitby, the car choked up each hill to nudge the edge of the cliff – even if we didn't make it, we could verify vertigo. Hold the wheel at ten to two, you said. From Kildwick down to Cross Hills, Priest Bank was steep, the August moon hanging low in the trees. The world darted in and out of view. At the bottom, the canal swallowed the image of the world, returned a blank canvas. Change gear, you instructed me. The road pitched the car forward. There's no way we can turn back now. The only thing we can do is to push on.

Near endings: that tidal grey of your eyes, rainclouds colliding; the sound of a spade meeting a stone; a jar of brushes against the dropping light; in the next field, a horse in a zebra outfit. I think you'd have liked that. Crows drop down onto the parched grass: grass the colour of sable or sand. I am thinking about the circus, and the circle, which means both hole and whole. A clown throws invisible balls into the air to juggle them. You asked us if we wished to see something we had never seen before and would never see again. How could we resist? You broke open a monkey nut, palmed the never-before-seen nuts and ate them. In the next field, the horse is quietly coming to life, and always in the distance are the ancient hills in which we must all lose our way.

Is it that I must now seek you in artefacts? A king made of iron and glass and cement dust? A unicorn upon a slab of stone? I bought both of these, remembering the story you told us about the days before you were born, when God was making you. He breathed into your ear, the way the Holy Spirit always enters the body, and asked you what you wanted to be. You thought hard, cast your eye across the lake that was covered in dandelion seeds and craneflies. I want to be a unicorn, you said. God narrowed His eyes: it will be a challenge, He told you, but I think it can be done. And with His Godlike hands he moulded you from clay and spit. He was just fashioning your horn, right there in the centre of your forehead, when you saw some children playing in the trees. The deep, gold light of the summer evening matched their laughter.

Stop, you commanded God. And God stopped.

I've changed my mind; I want to be a boy.

A slat of light lit up God's frown. But, give Him His due, he made you human, as wondrous as any child that ever lived, precise and fierce and quick to laugh.

You're not perfect, God said, as He surveyed His work, the glitter of metal under softness, the nub of a horn still proud upon your head. Although, in fact, He amended, I think you have come close, after all – and He set you down into His pastures to run as free as you would dare.

What are the ways we might meet now, the words of greeting we might find that will remind us who we are again? Do we work harder to be more precise in another language? Would I know your paintings by touch alone if I were to close my eyes and be led to them? Or would I know them by the frames, in the way that in a gallery people spend more time reading the title of a painting than they do looking at a painting? Perhaps that is why you were always so reluctant to give your paintings titles. I believe I would know them by the arc that marks so many of them. Or the elegance of a line scored excitingly close to the middle of the work. It shouldn't work but it does. I think I'd recognise your paintings (by which I also mean your ideas, your insights, your thoughts) by the way you could pull off what should not be possible. That is how I greet you now, by finding that moment as often as I can.

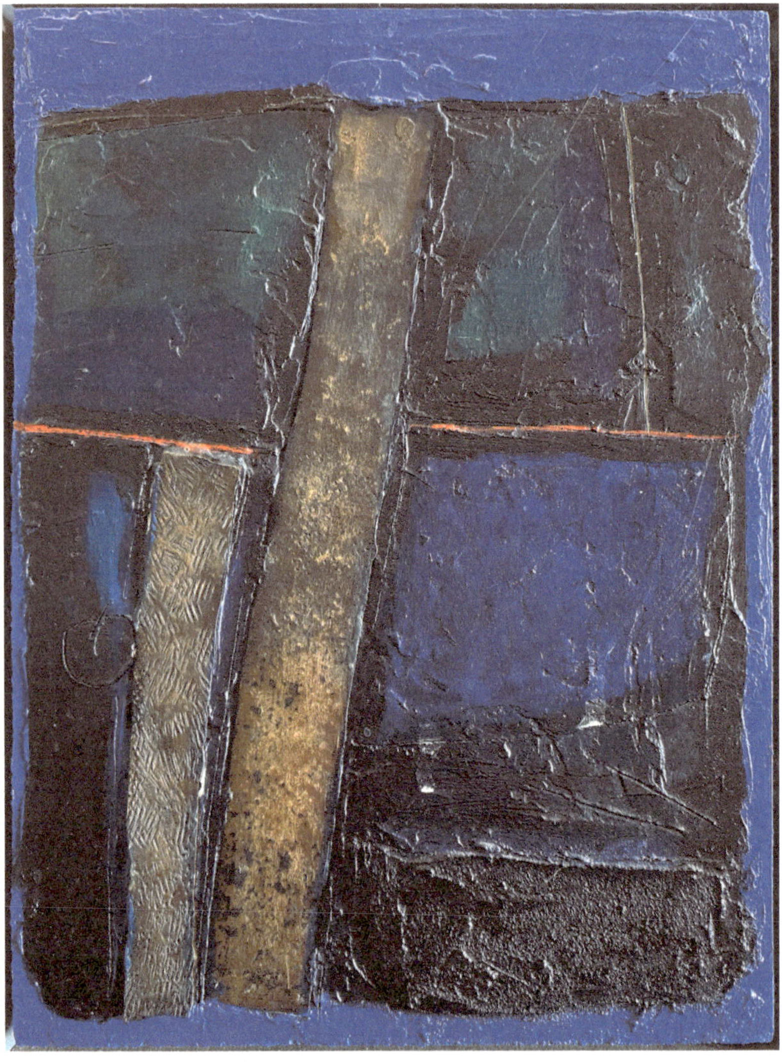

Shrine II: blue – the colour of the sun's penumbra, the colour of fabulous covenants: Afghan blue, the sort of blue Simone Martini sought and found. Blue lurching into rapture. Against this, two copper strips, hand-cut, reticulated. Ladders to the gods, still and simple. Now they figure the holy hill, the landscape as cruciform. Now they reveal a throw of the dice. Moving light narrowly outruns itself in a red line. It has forgotten it is connected to the earth. Soot black; perhaps the strips are chimneys, Blake's north. Plentiful black, against which everything shines and recedes. The job of the artist, you tell me, is to ask questions, lots of questions, and then make a space big enough for the viewer to find their own answers.

Shrine III Reflect: sand, cement, gravel, alkyd. The shrine is black-gold, scored with lines made by a flint, a knife or a chisel. Majorelle blue meets mars black. A copper panel is offset into a lozenge of ivory black; opacity: semi-opaque. If I look long enough at this, a mysterious radiance releases into an almost unimaginable unfamiliarity. The experience is mystically uplifting, quieting the clamour of the world into a single note. Perhaps two notes. Perhaps two notes and a third sound which is not a sound but an aphesis suspended between them. This black has the profundity of spilled ink on a pine table, black sinking to brown. Imagine bones charred to a cinder, the taste of a brass thimble from a button tin. This is the black of balsamic vinegar in an unlit room. The sort of black that shakes the throat of a bell-tower when the main bell strikes the hour. Just as the words for things but not the colours for them evaporated in your mind, this black is full of sizzle. A key gives out on my keyboard. The alphabet is shortened by one letter.

These two Shrine paintings hang together on my wall. No guarantees of anything but themselves. The word 'shrine' goes back to the Latin *scrinium*, meaning a chest for books. Here are the books of the earth, a mineral glow in the northern libraries of flint, millstone grit, soil. The world is never quite as given as it looks. Not to make sense is what matters. The understanding that comes from approximations nudges us towards the secret interior work of a painting, which is the thing that really matters. Reflect on this: what is seen might simply be its own likeness. Open the book: take notes.

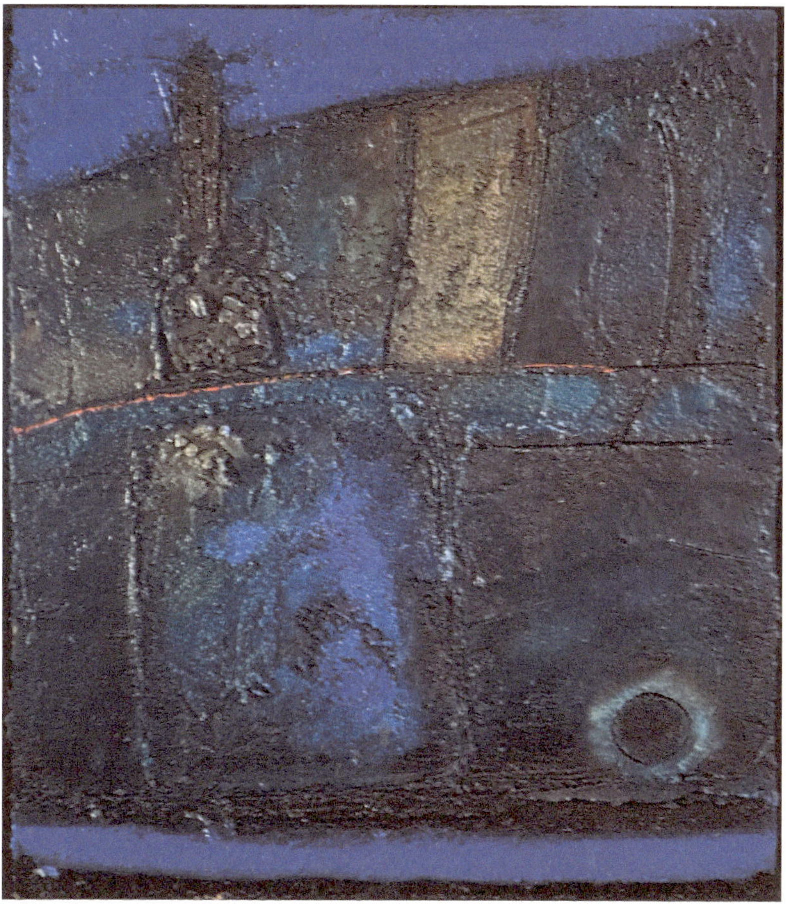

A fire at King's Head, bunches of burning herbs dropping from the rafters, the windows, fierce with orange and smoke. We ran through the house, banging all the doors, throwing towels on the flames. Freak mutations in time turned the staircases into an Escher painting as we tried to raise you from your bed. The air furled tight, then shed flakes of hot ash. A bang, a door, or a car backfiring in the street. Every window in the glass-house-workshop reflected and amplified the flames. I somehow couldn't grasp the present tense of things. We were lit from above and below. Brilliant spirals turning on an absent axle. You moved in a fever through the chaos and delivered us. I thought you were immortal, for want of a better term.

On the beach, stones blacken in the rain. The pier is a wasteland of chipped vanilla ironwork. An empty carousel of horses moves up and down. Along one of the groynes someone has painted: I'm feeling a bit normal today. The sea is shale and coal, as though the sea was the kind of earth a miner would recognise by smell alone. Gulls, backlit by the storm, scour the sky.

We build a rough pyramid of dark sand and decorate it with stones and gull feathers. It is an untamed good work, supple, indecipherable. It is as good as any painting. The wind whips sharp sand into our legs and eyes. You pull your winter coat around us both and that is the end of that. The next time we come here, it has vanished as surely as if it never was.

Things appear and disappear. When someone dies, time is flattened in a thousand dimensions. A film forms on the surface of the tea. Hard water, unsugared, strong enough to trot a mouse on it. A Madonna looks out across the ancestral landscape, her gaze strong, steady. Hours lose their meaning in the absorption of the work. The air in the studio teems with volatile oils and thinners and ideas. Is it that time of year already? It is nearly impossible to say what I am looking for, what I can dredge up now from the density of loss. Behind the Madonna, there are lines cut into a horizon. A pale halo of light eclipsing the day. What does daylight mean exactly? You offer us your example, lifted out of centuries of darkness.

There is something provoking about loss: the way the absence of a thing, or a person, screws itself into the mind and squats there. My mind won't accommodate it, but it knows its rights. I go over the same ground, looking for what I know is totally not there. I feel it as a mismatch between the chambers of my heart. They are locked in conflict against it. All that remains is the moment, emptied of you. Like everything.

When you think of it this way, there is barely any difference between having something and not having it. There is something brought vividly into being when I try to contemplate its absence. Look sharp, you tell me, but I cannot come, and I cannot bring any sharpness to the way I am looking. I am a long way away. Nevertheless, it is as close as I am likely to get.

A magic trick: from half a pack of cards, pick one; check it is the right one – the eight of hearts; not this one, the three of clubs; not that one, the five of spades. No?

Alright, but this is a disappearing card. Look, it has gone already. It's not in this half of the pack, and it's not in this half either.

Now, fetch a lemon and a knife from the kitchen. A perfectly ordinary, French lemon. And a knife, a *couteau*, if you will. Now slice the lemon in half. What's there, buried in the heart of each half of the lemon? Two halves of a cut card, tucked into the smallest core of the pith; ah, yes. It is that old disappearing/reappearing eight of hearts, fully restored. You'd have loved to have seen that. If only.

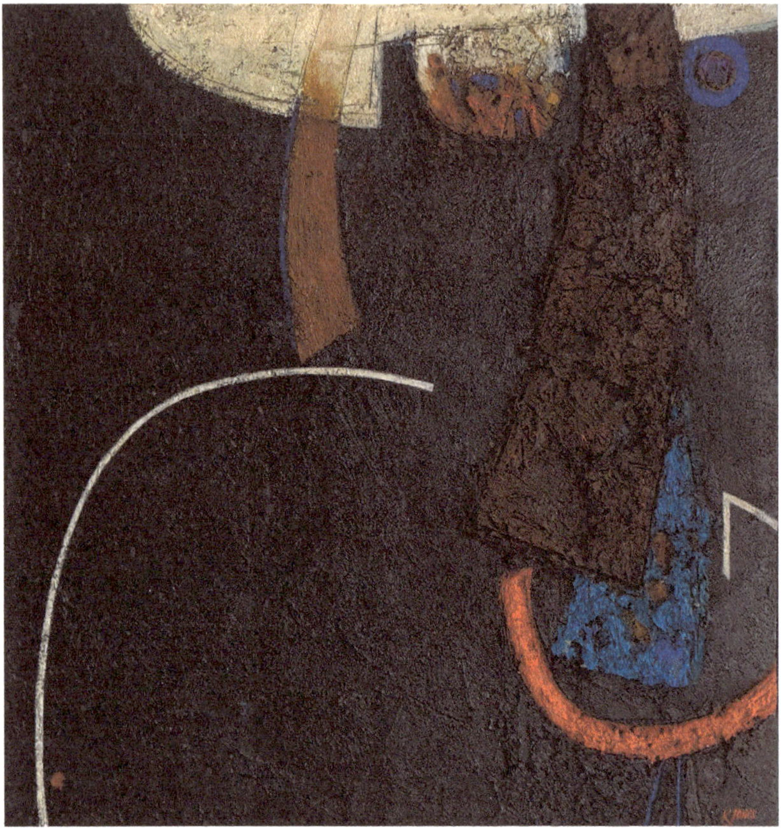

Alchemy I: the red paste earth: the effect of this red on the body is almost acoustic. Lead ore, called galena. The old lead mines above Gunnerside flake tiny particles into the soil, into the water that runs off the soil, into the air the moves over the soil. Lead is a legacy pollutant, which means it doesn't break down; it persists. Traces of lead in the groundwater, in the meltwater; the ground buckles under a century or more of industry, then gives itself back to nature. Tonnes of rock, scratched, cross-hatched. Mines, sealed into draughts of darkness, black shaded by stone. Bones, loved or not, also filter this. The dead buried in the dialects of the dead, which we can never hear now, although we must assume they are waiting, preparing themselves for resurrection.

A thought going out of focus, like a fret of rain smudging the line of a hill. The opposite of this occurred when you lifted a brush. The sheer bravado of using a wallpaper brush to paint with, affording you big lines, great sweeps and arcs. It's handsomely exacting. These are lines that make the whole body react to the painting. All my early memories are of forms and shapes and contours, overt outlines from the West Riding of Yorkshire. A road glowing under the brow of Kilnsey Crag, the individual calligraphy of the landscape. Art is the way we articulate what it means to be alive, you tell me. Seeing is a way of thinking, you said; that's why we say, the way I see it…

Life is not linear, yet it makes itself known sometimes by means of a line: a line crossed; a boundary; a border; a line made on a page. Sometimes the lines are mobbed by shadows; sometimes we can get into the groove. All the synonyms for line have something to reveal about how to live:

Example one: stria: a seam cut into a surface or, alternatively, any of a number of longitudinal collections of nerve fibres in the brain.

Example two: thread, from the Old English for to turn or twist: to see things from another perspective – life, inevitably hanging by a thread.

Example three: virgule from the Latin for scratch, twig or comma.

Isn't that wonderful?

Simultaneously palpable and ineffable: paint, face to face with itself. Under this, cement. Over this, an aluminium disc of gold, cut from a used paint tube. The paint tube was invented in 1841; before that, a pig's bladder had to suffice. The world is endlessly symbolic; one idea meets the edge of another. It is love that draws us into a painting. If you didn't love it, you would say it hurts. If you didn't love it, you would think it could offer you nothing. Scratches on the surface shine over scratches on the underpainting. Live longer. If I imagine you now in your box of soil, it is with a flint in hand, or a rusted nail, some sort of edge, making a line in the dark, seeking the place where everything deep is also shallow. It is a long story. We are dead a long time.

I think of the great respect you brought to your work: respect for the curiosity that provoked it, and for the tools at your disposal to discover it. Look again, you told me, which literally translates as respect. Look again – what do you see now? Light breaking the surface of the land. A dark, bright line which marks the horizon. Shafts of light, which can also be seen as darkness. If I reach out to touch them, it makes me shiver. I think of how we measure years in terms of light, as we head towards the final luminescence. There's no eyewitness for that, but look at Caravaggio, look at Blake; the work might invite us to reflect upon it.

I am not clear about how one thing leads to another, how a life spent on the edge of the known leads to a gravestone on a hill. I'm not sure, how after that, all the things you contrived to hold together in time have simply scattered to the unopened drawers, while you have gone to ground. We are not a family of planners; we make intuitive, arbitrary decisions prompted by curiosity and a sense of finding out. Nevertheless, once these decisions are taken, we bring an intense intention to make something, to bring something into being.

There is a line of silver rippling over the paving slab where a slug has moved, making its mark. It prompts me to think about the marks we make in a life: how deliberate they are, how unavoidable, and how transient. The trail is like a fairytale ribbon, enabling the slug to return from the forest. It is a line of communication: this is the way; I was here. I hazard this with some trepidation. Nevertheless, there is pigment in it, and persistence, and it shines across the stone, the way a body at work shines.

Hardly anything: a brush stroke of black the colour of poppy stamens, red-black; or magpie feather, blue-black; or devil's coach horse beetle, green-black. A study in uncertainty: ours to look at, ours to ascertain. Here is the black of iced tarmac, nudging against the warm black of rotting mushroom gills. Vision persists in asserting its margin for error. Black the colour of the stripes on a mackerel, stripped of sunlight, vanishing again. A tangle of blacks, slipped into the bottom left-hand corner of this painting, almost intricate yet too shifting for that. A blink and the passage recedes. Other forms in less unlikely places invite the eye to look away. Still the black, hardly anything, a brush stroke, calls us back and suggests it might be possible to start again from scratch.

And if not black, then red: wallflower-red, the red of cayenne pepper, the red under the black of a burning log, the tragic red of the letting of a boy's blood on a wet pavement. The red of rose hips, the reds of suns setting behind the city's pollution. This was how you attended to the world: laying down one colour next to another to make them both shake – or they could be dancing. Perhaps the day was light-hearted. No doubt pears hung on the tree, ready for harvesting. And now all those days of childhood run around together, giddy in their dressing gowns with the ladybird buttons, simple, just waiting to be forgotten.

There we were, standing at the lake in the clasp of the hillside. Before us, the lake drawing down the sky or throwing it back. A moorhen fanned out the water behind her. In spring you called the cuckoo; at night you called the owls through your thumbs and your cupped hands, and they called back. There was nothing complacent about this, it was a piece of sonic magic. And yet, if we go far enough back, there was everything complacent about this: Complacent, from the Latin *complacere,* to take pleasure in something together, to be very pleasing at the same time. How did we corrupt that into a word for smug? You hooted over the surface of the lake, and the amphitheatre of the hills translated your cry into echo: a series of uninterpretable, sumptuous vowels; nevertheless, something only you could make.

The things we consider lost: languages, opportunities, gardens, sense of humour, the plot. If I think of our lives as a series of stills, what comes up? A close-up of a taxidermied merganser duck; a view of Christmas trees in other people's windows in the speeding town; rain that is just too big on the tarmac outside the petrol station; a wet wind that smacks the scuffed railings at the seaside; sheep count in the old language – yan tan tethera methera pip – until it is time to sleep.

Back in the present, the Michaelmas daisies are out, starring the edge of the patio, like a tray-cloth thrown aside, embroidered by someone from your own childhood. The honesty has lost its plum colours and is turning white. A crow drops onto the lawn like an umbrella blown inside-out by the wind, then gestapos his way across to the apple tree. He looks like he should be smoking a cigar. All these things come together, in one moment, redeemed; simply here to comfort us.

There is a painting on my wall, with a series of structures across what might be a horizon line. Some of them are made from cement, others from copper pipes let into the board. Some of them have enamelled discs – like a coin at the bottom of a well; each one of them suggests the measure of us. Well, seeing is believing.

The apple, like the chalice, like the arc, was a signature. In the beginning was the apple, mystical fruit, rising out of rain and sweet blossom to make the air more luscious; in the pan softening into sugar. The apple: fruit of the tree of knowledge, fruit of the tree of temptation. Your favourites were the Egremont Russet, the Orange Pippin, the Worcester Pearmain, although the apples you painted were surely Granny Smiths. In your paintings they are falling, dropping through history to roll at the feet of Harlequin, tumbling from the still life of a house: the proof of gravity, and recklessness and trust. Until the seventeenth-century the word apple, or *malus,* signified generic fruit; potatoes were earth apples; tomatoes, love apples. The apple, the chalice, the covenant. Again and again.

Because you were, in spite of all evidence to the contrary, mortal, I call on memory to revive the times when you were at large in the world. In particular, the walk to Low Holden in the rain, with jam jars for sticklebacks or frogspawn. There were raindrops catching in the fibres of your gansey, and lines of black spooling out behind us from the pushchair wheels. In the middle of the field, the Owl Lady's house, surrounded by rooks in the high trees. At the centre of that house: the Owl Lady, dreaming her intolerable dreams. Her blood-daubed top, her fingers and thumb pinching the tiniest roll-ups. Her terrifying trances. I could never meet her magnified eyes, which were the palest blue, like fish themselves. We weren't looking for her, anyway. She would come out of the house and stand before us: part-sacrifice, part-belligerence, crumbs and columns of ash falling from her. She knew who we were seeking, but she would exact her measure of terror, just in case.

Those who never met the Owl Lady might perhaps conclude she was an impossibility, someone we exaggerated, like wishing exaggerates wanting. She was so strange and angry it shook the air around her. She stood unblinking behind her milk-bottle glasses and rattled our hearts, which jumped and missed their beats. When I think about her now, she still unnerves me. I wonder if the house is still there, not wanted for anything, turning itself into a relic. I wonder if it is as wild as Heaven now that we no longer walk the tracks that would take us there and bring us back. In particular, I am exaggerating the wishing for the tracks that return us, right as rain, and for the rain to be still sparkling in your dark garments.

The day you stopped teaching, you came home to take your turn at painting. You stepped out of our old Toyota Corolla into the middle of the road, lifted your face to the world and declared, 'if anyone asks what your dad does now, you can tell them he does sweet fuck all.' Across the street, old Mrs Clarkson scurried indoors. And that is all I remember of that day.

After that, everywhere we looked – ploughed fields, rock striations, graffiti on public statues, ferns in bridges, crinoids in stones, the white lines down the middle of the road – everything might be classified as art. After that, everything we saw, we saw with a view to repurposing it: limestone, millstone grit unfinished to perfection. Not much has changed. On my desk, a strip of stained linen has been sewn to a rain-botched photo. Rusted staples the colour of a young man's hair. Everything unique and apparently unrepeatable, and yet everything conducting an intimate conversation with everything that came before. It appears to be the truth. Then, to the left of all this, there is your face, looking up through all the glitches and foxings, as though you had drowned in all that art and were lying at the bottom of a pool of it, staring back out at me. Yet, how gallant these things are, that you have left behind.

I am sitting here in the lamplight, trying to still my thoughts enough that I can call you close. A clock chimes the half hour. Chances are it is time to talk about ghosts. At once, I hear the noise of the broken scooter going round and round in the coal dust in the cellar. I see the yellow rope turning in the stale air. At once, I feel the chilled weight of the greatcoat with the bullet hole through the breast. I treat each thing as laden with intent. How quiet it is. When I hear the beatitudes, I cannot help but think of May. I can smell the left-behind smell of her house. It's a reflex, or it is a shortcut to recalling her. When I hear Pentangle playing *Goodbye Pork Pie Hat,* I cannot help but think of the spiral staircase up to your studio at Busk. The painting of Punch, Lord of Misrule, is on its side, his elegant foot raised for the dance, tilting anarchy into tango. When you painted this, the impossibility of death was years from being imagined. Somewhere on the dark landing of another return staircase, your children are dancing as you – way out of sight – play the theme tune from *The Third Man* on an old piano. Well, I thought living with ghosts would always be like that: a sort of togetherness keeping me company; not exactly present, but persisting nonetheless.

A delicious, cold day, full of peach fire at the end, turning this room into a golden cave. It's hard to see your paintings in such a light, though it catches on the copper panels, and sinking lower, the blue takes on a faint pink-bronze glow. I shake myself awake, write some more. I think of Rilke saying that beauty is the edge of a terror we cannot bear, and I think it might be the other way around. I think of the attention you brought to that distinction between the two. The sky is royal, made of glass. I hold my gaze there, then I look away and there is this haze around what I want to think.

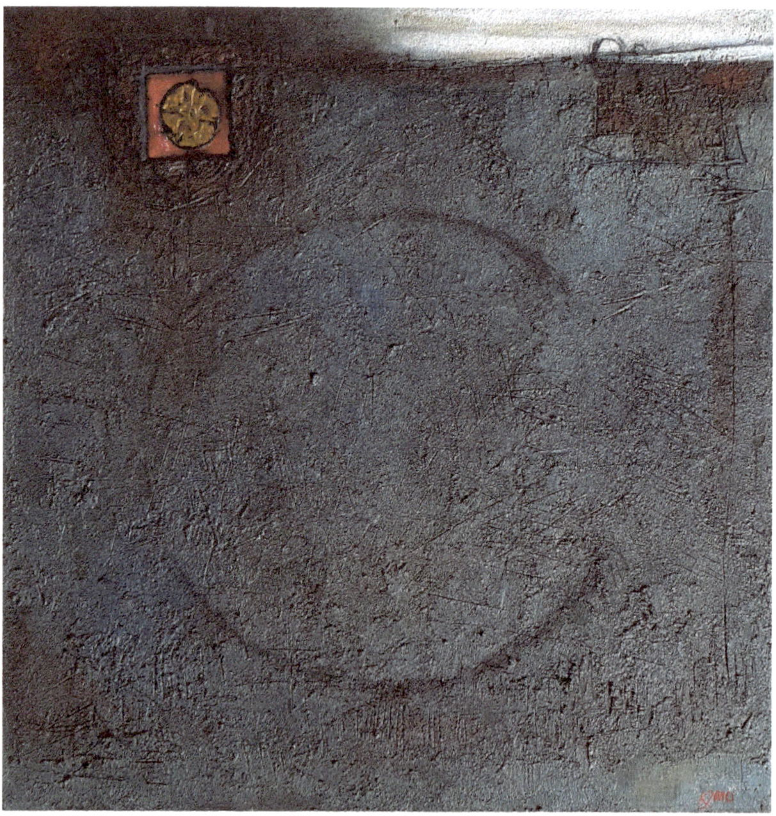

What is identity? The thing that categorically defines who or what we are, the thing without which we would be no-one we recognised. If you, Dad, are the thing without which I cannot recognise myself, did we *both* lose something when you began to erode? Is erosion even the right word. Maybe you were moving towards a completion – some angelic version of your identity? I look at the paintings and see the places where erasure is the important passage. Not just the layering of the paint, or texture, but the places where it is scuffed away. I consider these austere passages and know that what they have to say is important, skimmed with concealment, concentrated with looking. Nothing is settled; the matter will have to be looked into again.

Once upon a time there was a tree house affording spectacular views of the unexpected horizon. I am thinking about Kokoschka and how he said painting isn't based on three dimensions but on four. The artist is the fourth dimension. I remember you telling me about him painting *The Bride of the Wind* and the way he wore his lover's red nightgown and would not take it off. I don't know what happened to your painting smock. Maybe Mum has it. In the treehouse, the rooks and jackdaws entangle the wind: forwards, across, behind. A rope ladder swings below us. The wind is blowing due north and it is laced with delight; somehow, though, we have to get down from here.

There is a line that is not composed of a line, but of two surfaces coming together. This is both dynamic and very steady. It makes the kind of line that glances off being a line, the way a ghost glances off being mortal, maybe.

Hilary Mantel has died. There was a programme on the radio, an old interview in which she was discussing death and the role it played in her work. She reminded us that Aristotle says the dead are invisible, not absent, and she noted that of course they are still here in our DNA, our memories, our gestures, our inheritances. But she also said that when we wish to meet the dead and animate them, then we must turn to art. So, I am looking for you in these paintings that are so brilliantly necessary to my life. I just keep on looking, and then looking again.

I went down to the beck; stood outside the school and two houses from my childhood. The school is for sale. At the beck, beneath the leafy canopy of light, deer scrambled up the far bank, their incompleteness flashing through concealment and into the day. They made the space suddenly sunlit and dizzy. I was in the present world, and, also, I was in a world that was almost entirely constructed out of memory. How many days like this have I lived through before without registering them? How many am I living through now, that the future will wish to reclaim and hold tenderly? I never see them clearly; that is the problem.

I picked my way through the nettles and leaf-mould to cross the beck and climb back into Silsden. Someone had made two small cairns of stone upon a larger stone. Your words come back to me: all you can do is find what will suffice. I did try to do that today, but I think someone got there before me.

Sometimes I see an opening, a presentiment of what would or could occur if I could just keep my heart straight. I think of all the times I have sensed something on the brink of becoming real. A sort of inverted déjà-vu. I cannot grasp it but...

Out of nowhere, I recall the lollipops from Glover's Chemist: ridged oblongs of boiled red or green sugar on a tightly rolled paper stick. Maybe they were laced with vitamins? How else could they have been for sale there, or us permitted to have one? Another thing I cannot fathom is how memory decides what we will remember next. It is so random and yet so particular. Somewhere, behind everything I do not understand, I hear you playing the mouth organ, and my mouth fills with the syrup of the childhood sweet.

We chose you a headstone that I think you would have liked. A stone to stand in for you. There are certain famous stones – like the ones Turner painted at Lake Semerwater, like the standing stone circles in Wales – that I think must recognise me, I have passed their way so often, sat upon them, celebrated with them. She's back again, look who's here. I think if I had a stone for each memory, I could create a thing that would look real, though it might not be recognisable, even to those people who shared the memories. Christ called Peter his rock. What else does stone substitute for? Most of the time, it is just itself, and that is more than enough for it.

All perception is provisional, subject to revision, a guessing game, an opportunity for interpretation. If memory is sensual, olfactory, as it's reputed to be, and as I think experience bears the theory out, how would you paint that? Something aching and pure squirted onto the palette? The colours of this landscape: the grey of burnt cartridge paper on the wind? Soil under frost, river-water mixed with tobacco? Dank sandstone, blood blued with silver; the black of a tooth filling? Reds: lily pollen, iron ore, paprika: what do words come to mean? I am trying to jump-start my brain into remembering something truthful, or perhaps I mean real, about you. But the closest I can come is the turpentine scent of memory evaporating.

The evening is granular. Night falls. The lights go out on the paintings.

I wonder if the work of a painter is to make the invisible visible. The world is full of invisible things, the secret signals from one perception to another. A painting that lacks dimension cannot invite us into that space. A painting has to have passages of thought, textures that resist meaning yet prompt something close to recognition. The work has to exist within us, tickling our brains, even when we are not looking at it. In this painting, *Ritual Objects III*, there is a dark square, the black-green shot with the blue of labradorite. Across it is a line: a chimney or a ladder. Is this an interior? The shadowed shadow moving, like the shadow of a cloud being whipped across the lake; or the dark beneath a table laid with a green-fringed velvet tablecloth, lit by a lamp shining from another room. Another way of looking at this is to see a man with his arms held high to the sky, like the man who measured clouds, holding out armfuls of light.

The work is big, because there is a lot to say. There are colours glazed over other colours, new tones and insights, each one a miraculous reinvention of the palette. Always, there is something to be said for determination, and you probably said it. Now, I see things that I couldn't see before: these brush strokes revivify those conversations. I am invited by the work into a language I do not speak, but which is as significant and necessary to me as my own. It catches me unawares. There I was. I thought you would always be here. Now I am on my own, finding you, then losing you again.

Wherever we go, we gather great stones to prove the existence of time, or weather, or home. Here is the Saxon head, set above the doorway now at Blades. Perhaps that is its final resting place. Here is the Welsh granite headstone, in a limestone field that hangs in a valley above the falls. But time is not place; we cannot build on it. Nevertheless, these stones, garlanded in yellow lichens, show the conversions of light upon the places we hold precious. Home is not a monument, and yet its stones and structure weather the storms and the day's shine. Picture this: a family in a standing circle of stones, and all the crows of Wales crowing and beating their wings. I think I was a sulky teenager that day.

The crows are quiet here as the day is blotted by dusk. The trees creak gently, rising out of the violet, watery stretches of bluebells in the woods. I am already half-drenched in memory. If I half-close my eyes, I see a wash of ink in this crease or fold or fault-line running from the sky to the earth along the line of the tree-trunks. So much rain-stained darkness linking distances. When I look again, everything changes. There is just the gold of the house windows, and the good shape of sheep on the hills. How odd the lights are – it is hard to say which one is brighter, when you really look. There is a blue circle painted onto the trunk of a tree. If I lift my eyes and squint through the gloom, I can just about make something out there, ruffling the folds.

I wonder if before you left there was a sign, something I should have paid more attention to? I remember you telling me that the most surprising discoveries are made at the edges of things, and that when we make those discoveries, the glancing marvel of them momentarily recompenses some of the world's disappointments. Then the real work of encountering the thing itself can begin. Often it begins with a line, you said; just a mark. It's about knowing where to put that on the page. It's about seeing the blank page and knowing exactly where to draw the line. So, I keep making the marks. A child draws a house, and larger than the house, the people. I think of the houses we have lived in, those houses that composed the landscapes around them, blunted by the weather.

Memory vanished, and you were left with the empty present. Though not exactly empty; it was full of misfirings, complicated obligations and flashes of humour. The world was constantly surprising and frequently provocative. The light threw a lilac shadow across us. It weighed nothing, or maybe next to nothing, hard to say, and then it moved on. Are memories like that? Their presence seems weightless, until they vanish into a featureless infinity. So much of what makes us who we are is made up of memory. How was it possible that something so exact, yet so mercurial, defeated you? When you picked up the brush, did you remember how it transformed you?

Perhaps whether you remembered or not is not the point. Perhaps the point is to be open to the transformation. To see the world in a grain of sand, for example. In the pocket of your coat: a book of Yeats' poems. In the pocket of your head, or maybe heart: whole libraries of remembered poems. Like all art, a poem brings us to something luminous, the moment where a word startles something else into being, just as our footsteps on the path startle the curlew into the sky in a flapping of alarm. What the poem prompts is not understanding exactly, but something more like recognition – an unknown thing that becomes known as if we had known it all along, and it is returned to us, like a prodigal sense of meaning.

The clocks in this house all chime different hours, each one gallant, or maybe flippant, in keeping its own time, circling each other and the day, resisting the idea that the present can move on. You stand in the ever-present moment, watching the wind move the trees, as it has moved them for hundreds of years. Happiness, or something closely related to it – a particular sweetness of thought – frees you from the things that used to blacken your mood. Perhaps, now that time is dense rather than long, and memory is fleetingly short, experience brings you to the same feeling of the eternal present that art did. Everything and its absolute opposite co-exist: dark is light; blood is stone; the beloved is a stranger. Neither of us knows what this means, but we each have our own idea.

How do we talk about a painting? I think it cannot be done without recourse to speaking figuratively, using the language of substitution and gesture. Trying to describe what something is like is to step into the world of instinct and memory. We draw on what we have seen before to suggest what we are seeing now. The honesty seed-head is a shaving of moon, masquerading as the holy wafer.

The way we see things is unique, individual, a perceptual signature. Sometimes things reveal themselves to us; sometimes they reveal us to ourselves.

Reading the uppermost passage of *Shrine IV* from right to left: grey, the colour of a pigeon's wing; green, a spoon buried in soil and then recovered; green, the sky before a storm; green, the underside of a nettle; green, a pebble from the south coast; grey, the light at the back of the sea; grey, asphalt; white, waterfall moving fast in and out of its bright cascade; green-grey, moorland under a thin rain.

But it isn't just the complexities of colour, there are forms here too: myriad signs and sparks. It might take me a lifetime to see each one and note it. Each one reveals to me the relationship between the way you saw the world and the way I do.

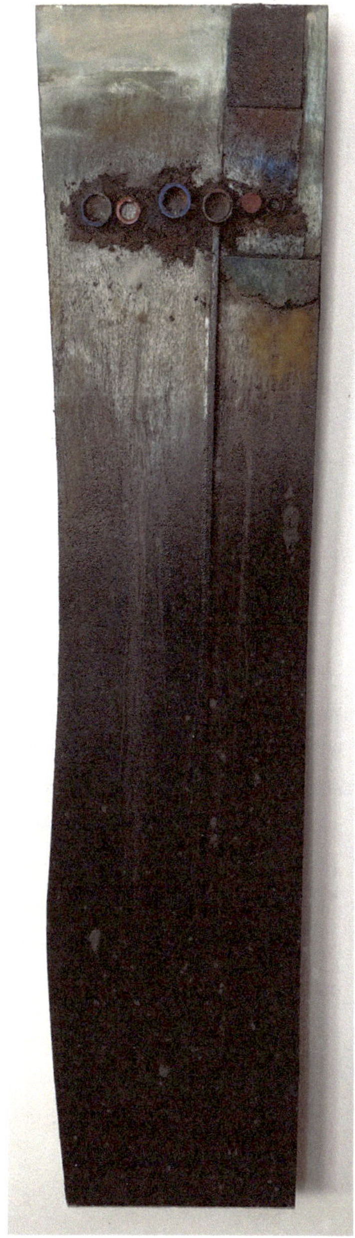

Stone on stone, half in view, half withheld from view. The things we make outlast us in ways that are unpredictable – even rusting, even pierced by the river's rush, they endure in the world. Each mark we make refers us to all the others in its constellation, the furthest light-sources of memory and association. It's how we make things mean something, just for a moment. Out of the corner of my eye: a shine of mercury, and your hand moving across the land, waving.

Here are the marks you made, so literally the same and yet in a time so changed can we really think of them as the same? Here are the words, written in your hand: imagination is the tool with which we experiment with possibility. On the tree above your stone, garlands of rowan berries and an iron ring, rusting in the sobbing light. How did it get here, this gradually eroding symbol of eternity? I wonder if this is how things always are, how they should be. And I wonder as well if it would be possible to stay here, making do with the stones in the field. Then I remember how much I like being indoors with your paintings, and I make my way back up the hill – but perhaps a little ghost of me lies down and stays with you.

It wasn't easy being a painter. You had to sneak up on the work, spending hours faffing, moving things around: brushes, skulls, ideas. Then you would take it by surprise, come fresh to it and grapple it into being.

Such things occur to me and they too are fleeting. Other things do not pass and maybe they never will. Having lived so carelessly with you, thinking we had all the time in the world, I discovered I was not exempted from heartbreak. It was a physical pain. And there is no reason why I should have been exempted, except that I thought love would not betray me like that.

Here is the canvas, as before. Here is the beck under Kilnsey Crag that I haven't stepped into since childhood. The day is on the turn, as all these days around the anniversary of your death are on the turn. There is gold, and red, a sort of brilliance reflected back at itself, as if an angel had appeared suddenly over the land, and then vanished again.

In the buried darkness where you now lie, are you at all aware of the music of the earth: the percussions of stone, one knocking against another as something inside you or beside you collapses? Does it turn your blood to water? Riffing on a scale that is so low we can hardly hear it.

Perhaps a century passes in the painted dark, giving rise to the shine of the narrowed look. There was a world that you moved in and observed, and then there was the world on a palette, a brush, a knife, a chisel, from which all marks must arise. The door is swollen in its hole. I suppose it's hard for all of us, getting in or out of here.

What does art do? It engages with the possible, and with the real. Your work was rarely drawn to what was already known, although you brought things into being that were just as real as an apple, say, or a sheep. Your work engaged with both the shifting nature of things, and their solidity. You worked with materials that were very present, present perhaps in ways that we have forgotten. Stone, metal, a handful of dirt from the land you lived in. The works bring these things together to suggest the passage of time and, as well, a kind of wonder that reaches inwards and outwards. Art is of us and we are of it. We are made of it, and to it we must return.

The story about wings that is the story about the failure of wings involves burning feathers falling into the sea; a boy, always a boy, flaming and falling. The story about wings that is the story about the success of wings involves a high window, four storeys up, and open; a child with home-made wings about to launch himself into the air via a make-shift slingshot, constructed from a dressing-gown cord wrapped around the door handle; a father's terror that his boy might spring himself into the burning air. How slowly you must have approached that seven-year-old.

What are you doing? you asked, as though you were merely curious.

I'm going to fly, he said. I thought if I could just get high enough, I could fly.

Far below, blackbirds hopped in the long grass under the orchard trees, pecking at the fallen apples.

Can you see those birds? you said. Look how they fly and then land. They don't have to climb into the tree to fly, they just take off from the ground. That's what you have to do to fly properly. You have to work out a way to do it from the ground, otherwise it's not proper flying, it's falling.

On this day: a curlew, winging it, faking a broken wing to lure us away from her nest. The day has got topside of me. I am aware of my shortcomings, my body with its familiar pains; my body, with its family pains: bone-ache, heartbreak. I can hardly recall how I came here. Maybe you rescued me from an oven-hob with childish fingerprints burned into the orange hotplate. Maybe you moved me out of a teenage sulk. Maybe you wanted to talk to me about the work you were doing, or thinking of doing. I look around for you; of course I do.

One minute it was you, scattering metalwork, paintwork, paperwork over the surface of the house; painting circles, drawing brilliant, freehand circles. The next it was the words cut onto Welsh slate: will the circle be unbroken? And on the air, your voice saying we never know how much time we don't have.

Imagine a man-shaped figure up ahead. Roughly your shape, walking uphill. The contour lines on the map get closer and closer but we cannot draw nearer to each other. Things only steepen. Imagine he is saying something important, but it is swallowed by the wind which translates it into something rushing and inaudible. Every so often, I think I catch sight of you, but the things you have to say are, you know, lost.

The sky is low cloud, green-grey, the colour of eucalyptus. I stand at the edge of the moss lawn, under the first big trees of the wood and I have no idea where to turn.

I wonder if all the words for things that we have lost or given up, extinct languages and ways of thinking, hover there in the air. Is it possible to think without language? Even the oddest thoughts only happen through words, so I wonder if you just stopped thinking when your memory went, and what happens in the head when thinking stops.

The only way for me to answer this is to think of all those drawings you did – and I did too, following you – intricate series of lines, each one echoing the last, flourishing like thought, like the brain itself, filling the paper with meaningless wonder.

After I failed my A-levels, I returned to school the following term by car; you thought that, at the very least, I could avoid the humiliations of the school bus. I made my way on my own. All the way down Priest's Bank to Cross Hills and back again via Kildwick. Rain knocking the windscreen, the landscape impassive, the classroom brutal. So much of your working life was spent in the classroom, living against the grain, encouraging bored and sulky kids to look again. There was the boy who cut every piece of paper into triangles; there was the boy whose socks had to be cut off his suppurating feet; there was the boy you threw against the radiator, for insolence.

For me, that was a year of living cooped up just behind life, the real life. Everything else was just a torn-out page falling to the ground, glitchy, dusty, the sun patched through the windows onto the scarred surface of the desk.

In the road, our sweet grey cat, half smashed, half poised to run, her fur a mess of red against the blue and white stretch of her interior. Her eye was glazed, but she was purring as if in shock at being still alive. You dug a hole for her a few days later and we laid her, wrapped in a towel, into a pocket of the earth, coarsened with grit and stones, fallen leaves, a scrunch of silver paper. A thin rain suited the mood, which was sombre and chilled. I don't think we buried anyone, person or creature, when the weather did not accompany us with its own howl. Her life was done and I laid her in the ground myself, but afterwards I refused to believe in her death. Half a century later, I feel the same way about you. But your life was not done. Your work remains unfinished: a thin, bent line of scarlet against a copper blue; some underpainting, the gesture of a shape barely sketched out. When I return to the house, I lie cheek to metal in my copper bath, and I let my mind go blank.

Zigzag: the road to Stalling Busk as seen from above, shining in the rain. Zigzag: the word itself moves in two directions. The word is young, its first recorded usage in ephemera from the 1600s, from the French or maybe the German for point or jagged projection. As a line, it doubles back on itself, but moving forward it offers the shape of a heartbeat spooling out on ticker tape. You saw it first; I only recognised it after you had painted it. Zigzag: something snags at my erratic heart.

We are drinking a Jack Rabbit Shiraz in the handblown glasses you were given for your birthday. You recognise the image immediately, in the way that now you do not always recognise a face. That's not a rabbit, you tell me. It is a hare. We swallow a mouthful in unison, perfectly in time.

The difference between a rabbit and a hare is that a rabbit is born naked in an underground burrow and a hare is born covered in fur, in a nest above ground. The landscape around us rests quietly above a maze of warrens and nests. Everything that seems like solid ground is hollowed out beneath us; it could give way at any moment and we could fall through into another dimension. There was the day we dropped down from Burtersett, on the road above the lake, to see two hares boxing in the field. There was something miraculous about that.

An unexpected gully opens up in the conversation and you stop mid-sentence. More wine, Dad? You look at me as though you cannot comprehend the question, nor who I am.

Earth palette: ochre, Naples yellow, burnt umber gamboge, phthalo blue, lead white, ruby madder, alizarin. The arcs: a chalice, a rainbow, a horseshoe, a breast, each one of them a different way of saying I promise, a different way of saying lucky. Always, the heart reaches for something beyond itself. Now the landscape grows old around you. Star moss, lichen, stone.

Heaven palette: a cloudburst and rain dripping from the hawthorns. Prussian blue, flake white, cremnitz. A single berry in the rowan tree. Heaven is metal on metal, a struck tuning fork of blue, the edge of memory. Imagine a single line falling all the way to the horizon.

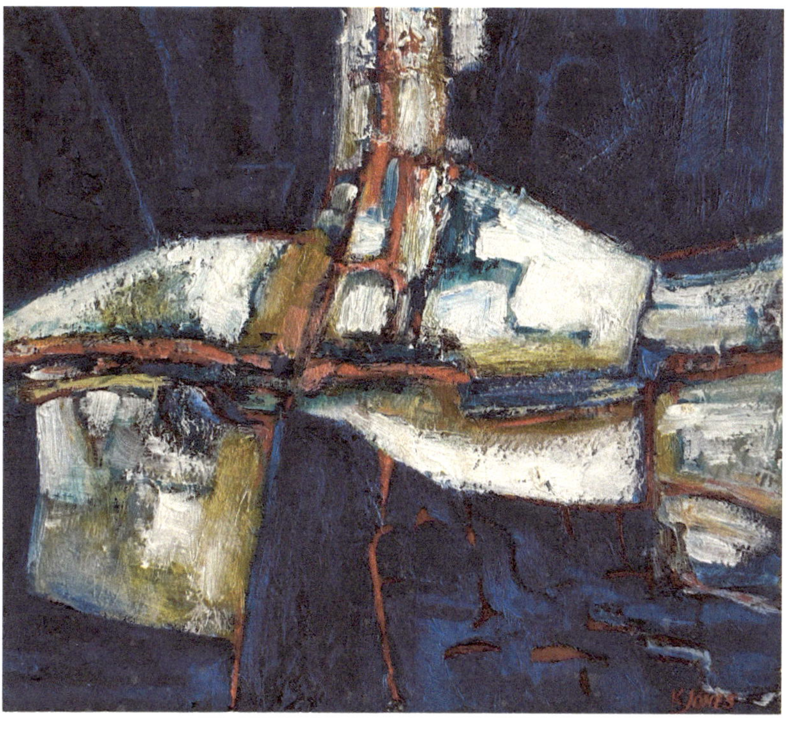

I am thinking about Rauschenberg's white paintings: pure surface. If you look at them long enough, you told me, you will see shadows and reflections; they have about them a kind of absence which is more like a presence. Were you guiding me to think about absence differently? To look again and see what I was missing? If I look at the surfaces of your paintings, the textures rather than the forms, they are pure depth. It is through the heart that we see the beauty of a thing.

As a colour, white is volatile, unstable. It is either too much or too little. It dirties quickly and spoils like sheep's wool, easily marked and sullied. Place one white against another and it looks black. In the tube, it is this thing named white. Once squeezed out, dispersed across a surface, it becomes something else: the pristine chill of a cheekbone, the glow of snow, the highlight in a field under the rain. In the process it has gone from substance to intimation, attribute and atmosphere. For centuries Foundation White, made from lead and titanium, was used for priming and underpainting a canvas. Wittgenstein distinguishes between two kinds of colour: colour that sits on the surface of things, as paint sits on a surface, and colour which goes right through something, becoming inseparable from the thing itself. It strikes me that this is the difference between a picture and art. Art occurs when painting transforms the medium into something lively. It is painting that gives colour the ineffable sense of movement and breath.

A day begins, a day ends. At the beginning, we know nothing. At the end, we know nothing. In New York, a painting by Mondrian has been hanging upside down for seventy-five years. It cannot now be hung the right way up because the adhesive strips which form its image are hanging by a thread. If we invert the painting it will collapse. Its story is a story of seeing things differently. Look again.

In Blades Cottage, a painting by you has been hanging upside down for over ten years. It works better that way, you said, although you refused to move your signature to the bottom right-hand corner. For my Christmas present this year, Ruby gave me the image of one of your paintings printed onto glass, and hung, upside down, in a triptych of images that also include one of the sunset on the day you were buried and one of you disappearing. The image of the work is inverted, the chalice converted into the sign of a promise. From now on, you are tucked upside-down into the cold horizon. Everything we thought we knew for sure is upended.

Did you forget how to look when you forgot how to recognise?

There was a change in your eyes as your memory deserted you and left your vocabulary to land where it fell. Your eyes seemed bluer, but more puzzled, as though the verb to look had fallen out of use. I've seen this in other people who have dementia. A sort of bewilderment, as though everything that language tamed had suddenly returned to the wild. What happens to the world of things when the words for them have shorted out? Do they become just flashes on the retina, the kind of floating visions that disappear as soon as you try to look at them?

Gathering the elements: a small jug, painted tenderly; a blunt-nosed face, impassive; a furnace, cinnamon-red; an insect flattening itself on a window-pane. Something, or nothing at all. A tin full of brushes and another full of turps. On the easel, a surface scratched and scratched again. The surface has to be marked. The windows in the studio are made of old glass, which distorts and shakes the view. The light coming through is straight from the clouds, falling first through one chute and then another. In the corner, a blue jug, glowing softly.

No need to pull all these things out of their context. Somewhere in both our memories there is the freezing kitchen at The Gables and the smell of sweet Clan tobacco on the frost-bitten air. There is the sound of a needle left to run on the record player and the tap water running cold enough to hurt our teeth. Here is the door to the cellar, and the light down there that is straight from a prison. Here is the lost drive under a tangle of briars and ivy and bindweed, leading to the bent iron gate we never knew was there. There are the peonies dropping their crimson petals. Here is the drive where I fainted as you reversed the car out of the old stables at what sounded like top speed.

In the hills, a slanting rain and the loss of texture that comes as the clouds cover the high dale. Dog weather, shaking its sopping coat into a shower of raindrops. Diesel melts on the road, a dark gleam of rainbow and rain.

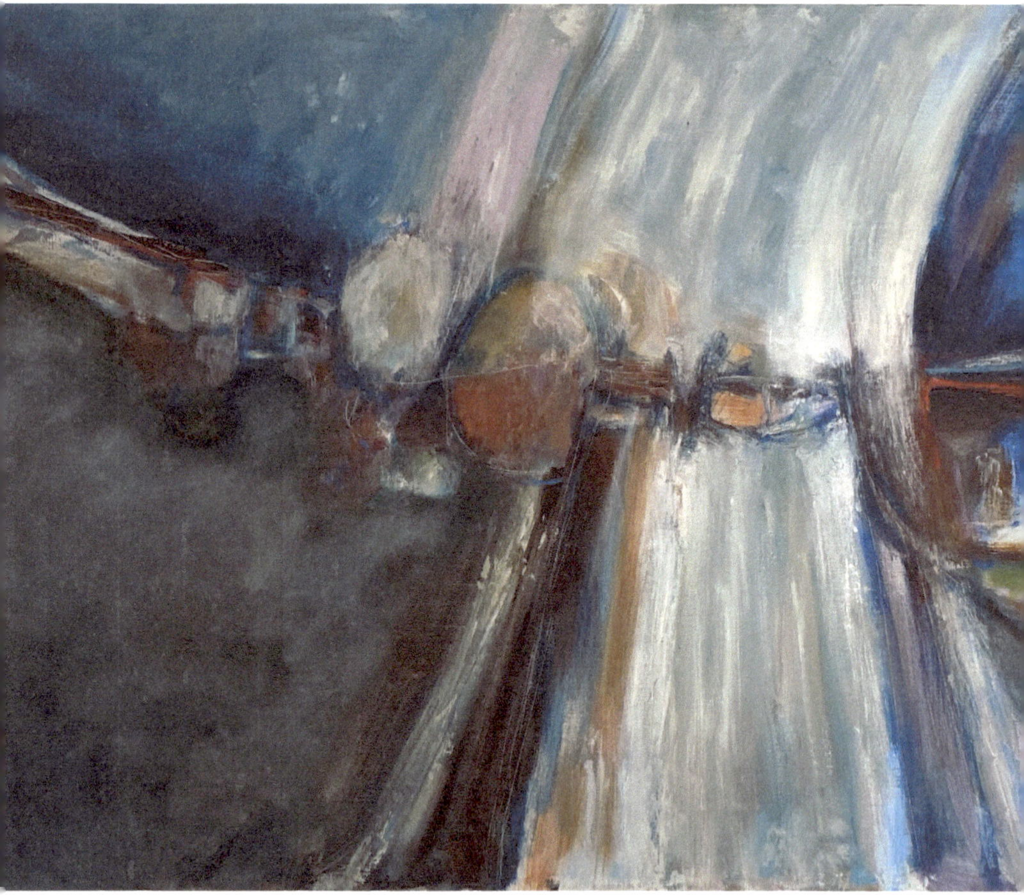

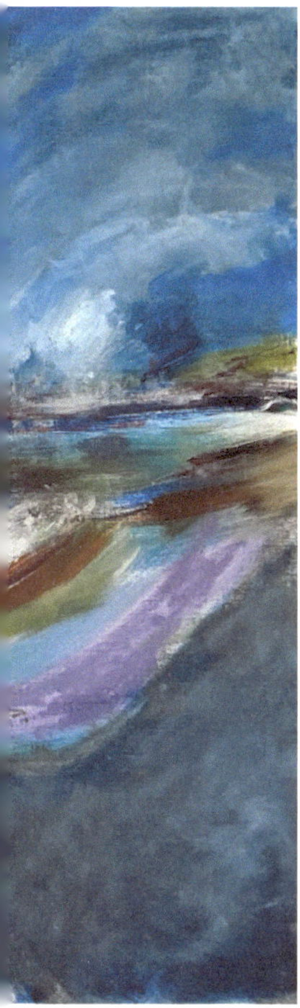

You hold a licked finger up to the air to show me where the wind is coming from. You point out the stars to show me how to find north, although something in my brain or in my blood feels like it already and always knows where north is. Our shadows as the sun sets are larger than life, reaching to a horizon we can barely imagine. In the late summer garden, you rub lavender, lad's love, lemon balm between your fingers and thumb and lift the warm scents for me to smell. Did you know it would transport me right back to you, years after you had gone? The garden as time machine. I have a photograph of your shadow, but although the sun still picks out my shadow, throwing it across the fields towards the circle of pines at Lady Hill, you are beyond the light's horizon.

Rain-lit northern stone. A crack running through it that might be a line of pure curiosity, a line that takes us out of ourselves. In the studio a bevelling, or not, of surfaces. The line remade. A square of gold, pierced fourteen times. A blue the blue of whales, which believe it or not are actually blue, the way the ocean is blue.

Days of rain and gold. The sky is a block of warm white with a stroke of cadmium yellow mixed in. When the sun drops it is like looking into the kiln, seeing metal softened by fire at the heart of the furnace. Meanwhile, I make small marks on scorched pages. I collect tiny bottles of ash. I pore over photographs of people I do not know, inventing stories for them they would not have imagined. Rain: darkening the glass, throwing a dark glitter at the window. Gold light: flame, a taper made out of a rolled-up photograph. I tear a photo of two people in half, then mend it with a little gold paper: photographic kintsugi. When the light hits your painting, it adds a line of gold that was not there before, a line that vanishes slowly, in just the time it takes me to have the thought that it is art that brings us more fully together, repairing the ruptures, bridging the distance between us.

I made a stone monument in the mountains: three stones for you the creator: artist, enameller, maker of all things from bread to gardens to family. If the wind dislodges them from their place, takes them downhill, maybe they will end up in the river, slipping into the clear waters beneath the apricot trees. I have made similar monuments in other parts of the world. When it rains, the stones will grow darker, blunter, incrementally smaller. When the wind blows over them, the air will be recomposed with the smell of them.

The M1, northbound, in hours of hammering rain: red tail lights shudder into water; the tyres barely connect with the oiled sharkskin of the road. In my pocket, a copper oblong of flattened piping, bent out of shape and purpose. We love copper, rescue it whenever the world throws it at our feet. You taught me what a good conductor it is, how easily electricity passes through it. It is surpassed only by silver. On my wrists, bangles of silver. Copper leaves a green tidemark on the skin, but protects us against seizing joints. The windscreen wipers sweep their relentless reversals in a sort of percussion; car tyres spin backwards. To my right is a concrete line, placed there to impede our crash into the next world. Gaps appear and vanish, each one a chasm. Like memory, hard to grasp then suddenly, frighteningly close.

What does dementia do? It leaves you adrift in a world of nouns. Or maybe it removes all the nouns and just leaves you with the abstraction of the thing itself. It is not named; it just is – but what it is, is mercurial, unfixed, unfixable. In the topmost garden you fork the earth, turning it over. Like language, the soil falls through your fingers: unpredictable, transformative, no doubt seething at levels we cannot comprehend.

On the envelope, a widge bird; in fact, several of them, signalling a different kind of movement. Little widges under ungamabrellas; little widges under rainclouds. I open it gingerly, taking care not to smudge it, taking care not to ruin its message, which is a kind of memory: this happened and we loved each other then.

No use waiting for the world to give me a clear direction. I must head into it, experience its dazzle and its drift. And I like to do that. I like to get under the sky. The little road zigzags left of the lake. Again and again, you meet me in this landscape we are able to call home. Again and again, I meet myself here. What happens to the work now that you are part of the land? Sometimes your grave is just a thing witnessed by me. Sometimes I fear it. Sometimes it shames me. Sometimes I am comforted by it and it lifts me up. Sometimes I can't even see it. Very often, I have the feeling I have gone the wrong way. But maybe I can't go wrong.

Lake Semerwater, the birthplace of the sky, and nursemaid to how fast it changes. The wind quickens its surface; the weight of sunlight turns it into half-polished brass, something scarlet in the gold. Here is the place of weddings, a baby dressed in black net carried in your arms. Years later, I go there in a red dress to stand in the water. As the sun drops, the lake chills to a flittering stillness, oily in the slanted light. There are sunken villages here, if we go by legend. Like memory, the lake draws me back to its irresistible shores.

How particular things are: peculiar in selection, yes, but also in detail – and also particular in that they are demanding. In particular, the horizon an ochre line disappearing into a yellow sky. Just looking makes me reel, or do I mean real? Against this a blue, almost violet lozenge, scarred and scored. The light is oyster over marigold, something golden but tarnished. There is a marvellous geometry to this painting. Ancient signs, erasures, revisions. Blueprints for tables perhaps, or a bird's wing. Fledge.

A shelf of brushes, stones, the skull of a ram. I am a child standing in the way of the doorway. It's forbidden, and my presence changes the room, breaks the moment, charging the atmosphere with something uneasy and fresh. On the easel, the huge painting, so large it will need a wall to be specially made for it, is transformed by the addition of Indian yellow. In the light of this, the dominant black of the rest of the painting – black the colour of old blackout curtains, black the colour of coal – streams with white to break the illusion of blue. On the turntable, Anouar Brahem is playing *Blue Maqams* with Jack DeJohnette, Dave Holland and Django Bates. Your brush is loaded with a light that is more like darkness. The jazz riffs against the rain. A quartet of experiences: paint and weather and music and the idea of me on the threshold of standing with you.

It is like turning compost. Every so often we go back up to the studio and pull out the great drawers of the plan chest. We go through things, lift what was buried to the surface, discover the great work that has been unfolding in the dark. There are watercolours of the *Commedia*, three or four works on paper of great vitality and limpid strength. The thing that characterises watercolour is its weightlessness, the white page floating underneath. It is volatile, mercurial, made for the insubstantial, the distant, the remote. Your players dance across each other, like mirages, appearing and disappearing, surfacing and vanishing from memory. The drama unfolds, withholds itself, replays and comes teasingly back for an encore. There is such joy in these paintings you had consigned to the drawer, as though you anticipated, when you painted them, the pleasure of rediscovering them.

There is so much texture to the world: lines, scratches, layers, marks, shapes. If we think of colour as texture, then colour also belongs in this list. Dominating this painting is a vessel cupping the void, finding it replenished. Everything is precarious, yet robust. Suns burn out, stars fall to earth, the chalice collects all the debris and transfigures it. I keep looking to try and catch the moment when something rises to the surface, emerges, comes into focus. Then recedes. You throw me a line, lighter than air. It is an entrance, or an invitation to an entrance. Come in, it says, and it opens its arms wide to receive me.

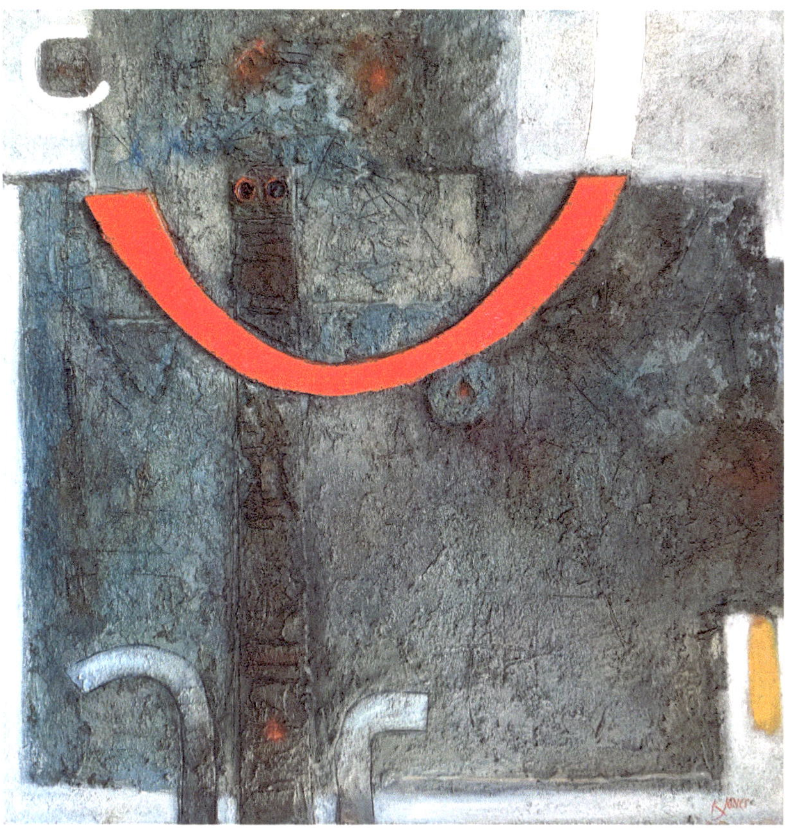

What brings the angels to dwell with us? A humble petition? A suffering human? It is possible to substitute art for ‘the angels’ here. I stand in the quiet of the studio, a quiet which is more absence than quiet, and these questions rise up in me as I try and subdue the longing I feel for presence. The only thing to do is to attend to the work, and I look for the first time, properly, at the mighty arc of the painting that typically hangs upside down. I always thought the arc was painted, and it is, but from this angle it looks like a blade of rusted metal spliced in under the paint. Like Thomas, I reach out to place a finger on it, to test how real it is. And I marvel again that you could have made such a thing. I am looking at about an inch of this six-foot painting and the angel in it rises out of nowhere and blows me away.

A steady rain, falling in cables of light across the hills. We are drinking coffee and talking about your work, the thing which demands and arises out of attention. I think of the paintings in which you created alchemical alcoves for things too high or deep to see, things which might vanish altogether were it not for the will to look again. What a risk to bring such gold or rust to bear. The rain turns itself inside out and the afternoon lowers its colours.

Eccentricities, dipping concentricities, circles within circles within circles. In this painting, a series of irregular rings is arranged across the width of the canvas. There is gold clipped with granite; something red and broken, like a pomegranate cupped open in the gutter; a copper pipe which passes through the heart of the painting, extending out of both sides by about a centimetre. There is blue, the warm phthalo blue, which owes something to the gallantry of green; yellow the colour of antique piano keys. A sun, perhaps, in the place a child would draw it – top right-hand corner – throbbing, all the colours of a rose, from *boule de neige* through to rosehip. The chalice supports all this, and more. In one of the apertures, deep set, an enamel face looks out at us, affording us a shiver of recognition, just a scratch of gold over white.

Above you, a rowan rattling in the wind. The soil stiffens around your cardboard coffin. No doubt the world's creatures have already reduced this to loam, and your good suit too, until there is nothing left but the gold of you to shine through the dark of silt and earth-drift. Your paintings are a lesson in how nothing has sufficient edge that we could grasp it fully. Love's vessel blurs its suggestions of charcoal, verdigris, burnt umber: now pigment, now ash and light, now brimming with implication. What remains of what we knew as colour is newly revealed in the unique light of this day, rising up from or resting into metal, revealing what it might mean to be everlasting.

Here is the story of a landscape on board, built up with sand, cement, wormcasts: lines which might be coastal margins, airy ellipsoids, contours of the abyss. The dark is fully immersive, not just an absence of light. The upper registers of *Small Totemic Structure V* seem to brim with uncompleted rain, irregular dots along what might be the skyline, or might be another rise in the land. The dark shines and the gold shines, for there is gold here too. Beneath the shine, the line is buckling. Beneath the buckling are all the histories we have not yet uncovered.

When I was two, I drew you a picture of a man and a flower and the sun shining on his windows. There was a horse too, but I hadn't drawn that yet. Were you aware how much, over half a century later, I would want to see this, your faithful writing down of my story to accompany the drawing? There must have followed more small accomplishments, more explorations and delights and more than all of those, a nod from you, behind the blue of pipe smoke, to appreciate the thing that emerges out of curiosity that might otherwise have been overlooked.

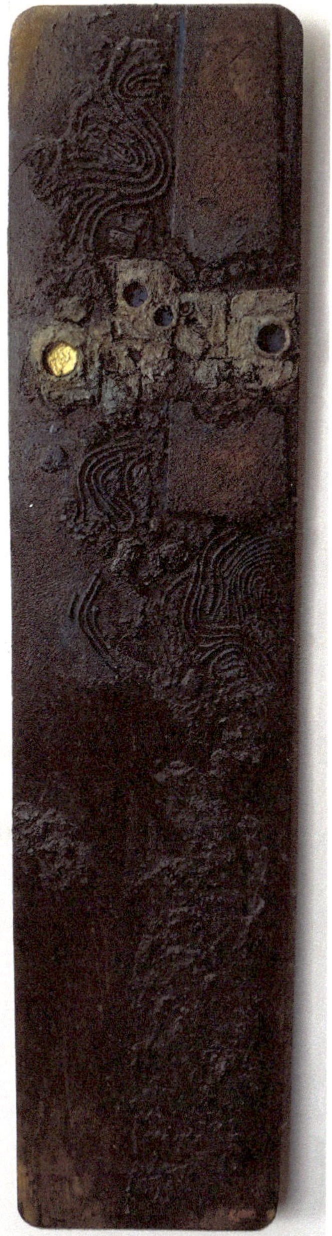

Of all the heart's mysterious devotions, perhaps the most subtle is the relationship to art. It is a relationship in which we are forever returning to the beloved, amazed; as though the journey to art were itself a labyrinth, and, at the heart of it, our encounter with the work constantly shifting. Again and again, I return to your work. The painting's textures both draw me close and close themselves to scrutiny. There is a kind of vertigo to it, and a dizzying uplift in which something is made simply and abundantly clear, and then the clarity vanishes and into the space of its vanishing drops a sort of desolation.

I think of your mind going out into the world to seek its objects: a flake of rusted metal, from the edge of a drinking trough maybe, from the side of a rattling trailer; a heart of flint, sapphire grey; a marble with a blue rope of colour twisting at its centre. I find myself groping around in the light, trying to find the things of the world, turning them over in my hand to see them the way you might have seen them. Right now, the dale is no doubt flooded by moonlight: the last full moon of the year shining down, the frost as thick as snow on the ground, and if I were there, straining to hear what you had still to say, all I would hear would be the endless crash of the Falls, falling.

A day of frost under white light composed of scorching brilliants. Spider's webs and ivy are edged with Russian furs. There are no shadows to step into; there is an elegant insufficiency of shadow.

Later, when we are drinking old port and the sun is setting across the valley in a wash of scratched gold, I look up and see two of your landscapes facing each other. I can hardly read them from this distance. The little road though, looks like it succeeds in a perilous space. I have to look away. There's another painting of yours, a bigger one I'd like to stand with and pay attention to. And that's not possible either. Nevertheless, I keep coming back to these as I think about the demands of art, and how they might be met. Behind me the light goes briefly rude, and then black. It seems I have finished my drink.

One turning, then another, then I'm lost. I don't know how it works but it happens. Getting there takes effort. Although I know I am looking for you, you are already losing definition, like words scratched across wet sand. Memory loss is permanent. Nevertheless, there are things to find that I could not have anticipated: a perforated metal disc the colour of a draining board; a prism of light in a sluice of snow from the eaves; an old diary with your notes in it, incomprehensible now, just another set of coordinates but no apparent way of moving on from them.

Ganesha, remover of obstacles, discovers for me a trace of your voice in a recording. It is a sound that could punch a hole in the universe, a sound that has become a moment, at the brink of a self that no longer exists.

Tonight, I am informed, there is to be a Geminid meteor shower – a fall of stars shattering dark matter. Like thoughts articulated and then gone.

Ganesha, lord of the universe, orderer of chaos, brings every last particle and atom into the wild and safe space of the night. I plead for preservation, but that isn't what I mean. It's not preservation that I want but a time-lapse, just a moment when you, who said something that I might have missed, were live enough to say it again. I strain to hear. I can tell you what I didn't hear. But it took bravery to want to listen to it again.

Late smoke in weighted light: *White 2001.* The white painting, salts and tears. Opal lights swim before my eyes; blue roads shimmer on the cusp of collapse. The whites are lethal, heavy metal whites, offering the hint of a burnt skyline, pale copper, bruise, the white of unlit subways. I stalk the edges of the painting, looking for the opening into this landscape. As I get close, the surfaces give way and perception dissolves. It is like being on the high moor on Boxing Day, everything thinned by the wind. White oxides, white tracts, white silhouettes flicker against white walls. It snows or it hails, or there is smoke rising from the past. Another roll of the dice, and the distance between then and now rises, half-heaved up a slope. When we get there, we will be able to see everything.

I have been thinking about black and how often, as an artist, you would argue against the possibility of a pure black. Then you went on to produce that wondrous series of totemic structures, large sculptural pieces, mostly black, with tiny accents of jewel colours, sometimes enamelled, sometimes the burnished gold of a reversed paint tube. Maybe they formed a roguish part of that argument.

They provoke excitement, situated one shine above the level of doubt, as I move to join the discussion. There is so much texture to the blacks you make, the way they move in a rapt meditation on form, the way they relax into space. There is nothing fearful about these structures. They exist, changing the space around themselves, and they themselves are changed, as a flower changes when you dip your face to it to receive its fragrance. Everything blurs and becomes simultaneously more intense. Leave the meanings out of it; a painting is not painted to mean something, it is painted to be something. Any symbolism from now on becomes almost soporific as we murmur our way through what black might be made to mean, if a painting were to have to mean something.

The word carousel is from the Italian, you tell me, or the Spanish. It means 'little battle' and it was used by the crusaders to prepare for Turkish and Arabian marauders on horseback. I think of the galloping horses rising and falling, with the old steam engine music chasing them round. I think of you raising your hand as we spun out of sight.

From Asia, the aspidistra, cast-iron plant, so called for its ability to withstand cultural abuse. It can grow under conditions of the deepest neglect. I think of the parlours in which these plants grew, parlours which we called 'the house', as though the rest of the house were but an antechamber to the places we never visited.

Quantum: the smallest amount of anything. Take black, for example: add even a tiny dot and everything changes. Take light, for example: the simplest match banishes the dark for as long as it burns.

Twist, or double; double or twist. The stakes get higher, but in times of war, and domestic weather, the smallest amount of anything makes us reconsider everything.

How much deeper would the ocean be without sponges? I found a scrap of paper in your handwriting with this question written across it, together with an observation. It sank into my consciousness like something sparkling underwater, sunlit sand falling maybe, maybe oxygen. It made me consider the sanctified depth of the work of all the other things I fail to pay attention to. The rising moon last night was a low-slung, red-gold fairy tale, shining through the iced trees, a symbol that we might prosper as we emerge from the darkest heart of the solstice. There was joy in it, as there is in your question. And something hurtful about it appearing to be so close, and yet being so far beyond my reach.

Listen, my ears ring, and the sound sings somewhere in the back of my neck. There are wide open spaces for patience, if only I would step into them. The solstice approaches; maybe then it will be quiet enough and dark enough.

Naked, the world under snow. Paths edged with blurred stone walls, a line of black, or maybe not black, maybe crow-wing. All descriptions are precarious in this light. Naked, in the sense of not quite definable – it is hard to let the eyes rest upon the view. We thought we could buy a bit more time. We didn't think it would have to be bought. A blistering of hail pelts the vision into white shadow. Or maybe not white, maybe sheep skull, a next-to-nothing thing. The grass is bitter. I'm cold and it is all I can do to stop you giving me your coat. I compose myself into its rough embrace as it goes round both of us, and we make our lopsided way back down the hill, following the blunt line of the snow at the edge of the land.

The sky is momentarily Turneresque, molten golds and slate, before tiles of rain drop onto the motorway as I head north. Tail lights flare on and off. Infinite speed, but slow. I am beyond weary, beyond partied, beyond sleep-deprived. Fault-lines in my body give and catch themselves. The present is diminished – just two cars long, one car wide on either side. Afternoon light the colour of slush. It is almost meditative, out-of-body, trance-like. I can't tell the difference between moving and stopping. I remind myself what that might mean, and scrabble for fruit pastilles, water; I open a window, then swiftly close it again. Anything to make myself concentrate harder. You are beyond me, even though I am coming home. I cannot get you into focus. The car in front brakes again.

Glints that run through each other, music and the shining smell of paint. The church bells are ringing, which is a sound I like to hear. When I last moved house, I was sorry to leave the sound of the bells of St Mary's, but we arrived at the new house on a Wednesday evening in late summer and it was bell-ringing practice at St Peter and St Paul's, and it was as though the village was ringing us in. All year round, the sound of an iron bell calling the faithful across the fields and villages and parishes of Britain. The gentle turning of the calendar that you must hear – at some cellular level – from your hammock of earth just below St Andrew's church. I have never disliked the call to prayer, at whatever hour, in whatever culture. Above almost any other sound, it makes us aware of the silence that surrounds all sound, and in which peace, or at least comfort, might be found.

Christmas time. Beyond the dazzle and glitz, and the mulled wine and carols (all of which you liked) the earth has turned again, and we are returned to the night of the birth, when God gave us his word, and the word was made flesh. As I look at the cards that depict the nativity, I see that almost all of them show the baby in the centre of the scene, a child from whom everything radiates outwards. I cannot recall who it was that drew my attention to the fact that the baby is the only human creature in that scene who both can and cannot speak. He cannot speak for himself, yet his words speak throughout all time. And this baby brings us closer to God, if we wish, but also, and perhaps more profoundly, we come closer to humanity: we understand more of what it is to be human, crying maybe, in the centre of creation. As St Augustine says, God is closer to us than we are to ourselves. There is something here about how I feel about my relationship with you these days.

Because we were promised snow and, instead, it rained; because the blackbirds and robins sing to mark the transition spaces of dawn and dusk each day, and they don't mind the rain; because Alexander the Great's horse was called Bucephalus and he tamed it by turning it towards the sun; because the cat has had a stroke, by which I mean a transient ischaemic attack, not a gentling, and his eyes look like he has seen something terrifying; because the snow was so bright last night and tonight it has all gone; because the flames in the candle burn orange as if there could be no other colour; because there is never enough time for everything, let's start again.

After you died, something in me dropped into a dark place, like the shine on the lake shuts down when the sun sinks below the level of the hill. Some adored thing in me went out and I knew I would never be that loved again. I began to erode. The person I was when you were alive had to shift to make room for the person I had to become, now that you were no longer alive. Sometimes, though, something of you inhabits me again, as swift as shiver. If I could call it up at will, I'd never be finished with it. There are times when I feel I might almost catch it, but perhaps I am simply tricking myself.

The signs of departure: a fleet of rooks lighting from the forest, hauling a fleet of shadows behind them. An alphabet, no longer recognisable to your hands after all those years of calligraphy, now just letters and a series of pure white intervals. Tiny, missable signs. A painful shoulder, an arm too weak to lift itself in greeting or farewell. A silver birch cemented into the earth. I stood at the window looking out, but all I could see was my own reflection in the dark, looking back in. We walked up into the woods, you knowing which tree was which, although you could not have said for sure who I was. It didn't matter who I was, for I was a part of you and we didn't know who you were either. But, look, you said: yellow archangel, thought to be an indicator that this was an ancient forest. Look, Dad, I said: huge trees – thought to be an indicator that this is still an ancient forest. There we were, man and tree and daughter, identifying the signs of survival and missing something, though we had no idea what it was.

Margaret came round, a dales woman, ninety going on seventy-two. She walks everywhere, is slight but strong. She has the brightness of meadow vetchling, but she is lonely since Tom died and she loves to talk. She admired your snowdrops. Yes, you said, yes, they are lovely. I think I'm taking some of those for my medication.

Mum asks me what I think she misses most about you, and I do not hesitate. Your unique, original view of the world. And she does, but it's not that. What she misses is your laughter, which surprises me – although we always did laugh a lot. And your side of the family in particular are quick to laugh, witty. Funny and dark. I do remember your laugh, but there is no-one now who has it. Dunc, who resembles you so much it sometimes takes my breath away, laughs like a different man. There is nothing else to do, but we carry on doing everything, as though life were an ongoing task, a way of proceeding into the never-ending. Or the everlasting.

Black limes in a silver bowl; water shivering in a pewter cup; chalk on charcoal. Painted and repainted, everything is held in this central embrace that has broken its banks. Its colours are the colours of life: soot from the chimney; white the white of old Brasso marks; the kind of blue outlined in grey that generally only makes itself visible in the human iris; the grey-green sheen of willow; cold marble; the warm brown of a calf's rolling eye; bright orange – the spores of filamentous fungus on dead wood. Each colour arises out of the cradle of the next, manifesting as arcs and intersections, colours moving between lines and echoes of lines, as simultaneously soothing and frightening as a lullaby. *Embrace: diptych* (naturally). The place where one thing touches another in order to prevent disappearance.

Landscape vertical, or: portrait of a landscape. Water pours through the land creating contours, traversing the undergrowth, loosening fragments scored with inscriptions. I see where your hand has been, sifting through possibility to arrive at the place where what possibility aspires to, happens. Old icon with a rose-pink halo, a blue robe. What is astonishing is how long it takes me to see these things in this painting of the land that I must have looked at a thousand times or more. Home rising up in the distance. Beauty is the least of it, and the very heart of it.

Art: Mine is to scavenge bits of the world and turn it into words. Yours is to cross the line, every time you lay it down. The world itself seems deeply indifferent, it carries on as though we were not locked out – although that is necessarily not the case. Everything we make adds to the sum of life going forwards.

The new year opens as a testament to time passing, a downpour drenching the windows, good whisky oiling the glass with a gold sheen. Here it is: a whole year, so far unblemished, blinding in its unexpected detail. What remains of the past, we take forward. A clutch of paintings, worm casts, badger setts, crematoria. Everything stepping back to clear a space for what has yet to become. Nothing will be lost, not a scrap of metal, not a slip of paper bearing words. Reflections of the past year shiver in the mirror. Call it, perhaps, a return journey: the new year coming round again. Everything new that you have to tell me I will have to find out for myself, from what you have already said.

If all painting, like all writing, is to a certain extent self-portraiture, here you are: flashes of gold in the dark that quicken and quicken again as I look. The night is cold, bone-clenching, teeth-clenching. These lines could be a fingerprint, concentric whorls casting shadows, making marks. Maybe too they are isolines: marks indicating steepness, something weathered, metaphysical, yet nonetheless rising from the physical. You deploy unexalted materials to create the body of the work, which is scarred, scored, marked with memory and insight. The perspective is unclear. Here is the work as sensational surprise; meaning is concealed and then released, scratched into the surface and then obscured, weathered and subject to the vagaries of time. It is no more possible to say of this painting that it is you, than it is possible to say it of any remnant, and yet, behind the surface, there you are: prompting the next idea.

Faith, and faithfulness. For a man who for many years was a determined non-believer, you had no faith, yet were full of faithfulness. Faithful to the work, faithful to the family. And you taught me how doubt is at the heart of faith; that faith means believing in something because of conviction rather than proof. Proof is inadequate to the deep mysteries of faith. In certain circumstances and usages, it is also a synonym for confidence, and maybe that is why people find it somehow both compelling and untrustworthy. You found your faith through testing, through striking a bargain with God. And perhaps, too, that is how you found your faith in the work. It's hard not to be blasé about something that sounds glib but is nevertheless hard won: suffering is what develops us. We become clearer through what we have suffered. Something unnecessary is stripped from us. It is essential to our flourishing; it opens our eyes to beauty, however imperilled or coarsened. I return again and again to the paintings and notice how carefully things are cradled.

So much that might be grasped eludes me, leaving just the dark or bright imprint of itself upon the retina. Quivering particles. Quantum physics suggests that art was right all along to focus on uncertainty, equivocacy, the shapeshifting ability of a thing to be itself and its own contradiction simultaneously. Of course, you can't focus on what is not there; you have to look again, look to the edge. Or into the centre. What is it like to die? To be emptied of all weakness, to be lifted into the space of full connection, where decades of being here expand into being nowhere? Blake saw the world in a grain of sand. What if heaven is the great richness of the soil, bringing us all together to feed each other? What if the greatest calmness of all is not light but the healing dark? Wouldn't that be peaceful?

I have been looking at the paintings and thinking again about boundaries: in particular, walls – the structures which protect us, which sometimes imprison us, which contain elements of our existence. How many walls have we encountered on our walks? As soon as we stop to look at them, we become part of them, in relation to them. We imagine what it is like to be them, in the great gales that blow through the dale. In the sunlight. Glints squint out of their surfaces. Small creatures, flakes of metal and strands of sheep's wool make their homes in the crevices. Rook feathers, blue twine, the same stuff as us, as life.

The important thing, you tell me, is to pay attention. It doesn't matter to what. You won't know what anything is until you pay it attention.

As you talk, you prod the compost-heap, just below the drystone wall, turning it and looking. Once upon a time all these hills were under water, a warm ocean. Look, here is a fish in the wall.

And, as if by magic, there is.

Out of nowhere, a memory of light falling like Victorian brilliants into the water. It was a summer evening, way up above Burtersett. We could hear the river rollicking over the stones to the lake, miles below. Beyond us, curlews pierced the blue dome of the sky with their cries; meadowsweet and kingcups softened the air. We threw ourselves off the rocks into the black water, and felt it close over our heads like a clout, and we descended forever. I cannot think about that day without a pang of regret. Like magic, it disappeared.

The world is full of story: the stories we were told as children and the stories we weren't told; photographs curling at the edges; misleading maps with roads that no longer exist. Everything is palimpsest, rescue, residue. One thing does not have to follow on from another. Logic is not as vital as magic. The object of art, you tell me, is not to reproduce reality but to create a reality of equal intensity. Giacometti said that. Which makes me think about his sculptures of humanity, figures so emaciated they seem to be mirages, yet still standing tall. Which makes me think about Antony Gormley's men, standing like watchmen or guardians, pinned to the sky. And then I think about the calcified figures of Pompeii: the tenderness and terror of them, and how there are some things we cannot tear our gaze from, no matter how long history lasts.

No matter how long history lasts, no matter how much of it there is still to endure, there are still all the things that sit to the side that have to be attended to.

Things that sit to the side: a moment's peace; five burnt matches; an auction catalogue; a tube of glue and a jar of honey.

Things that sit to the side: the bed, half-slept in; a book, half-read; the North Sea; the woman who waits for her dog to arrive. If the bed were a book half-read, which one would it be? The first books my eyes light on right here on the shelf are: *Counternarratives, Suppose a Sentence, Due Preparations for the Plague, All Mine.* The library readjusts itself. I thought I had a sense of my own life, but it turned out that for a long time, it has been just off to the side. No matter, the night cannot last much longer than any other mortal night.

A hymn has been going round in my head: *Immortal, invisible, God only wise, In light inaccessible hid from our eyes.* And it prompted me to think about invisible and visible, darkness and light. My thought was this: to perceive invisible and visible as opposites requires the body, an eye and a mind. The only difference between them is that one can be seen and one cannot. If there were no body, the difference between them would be eradicated. There would be no duality, only unity. It blew my mind: the vast superfluity of difference that we generate that distracts us from recognising what is properly whole. Maybe the distinction between burial and resurrection is only a matter of the human mind, imagining that meaning can only arise out of difference.

Perhaps, like the landscape, which was here before we were and which understands things beyond our ken, there are kinds of knowledge that we can't grasp. There are things the land knows that I do not. The wind on the moors is all argument. The sky is rushing away. In the woods, down by the canal, the Owl Lady is giving herself a home perm. The ash from her cigarette forms long grey coils, like the pupae of derelict moths. Her hair is twisted into newspaper and pipe cleaners, and treated with chemicals we dare not ask the names of. The canal smells of rain and the cold interiors of churches. We stand solemn, and apart. Indeed, we know we are nothing in the presence of all this.

We are nothing in the presence of all this; we are less than the sheep. They call to us, bleating into the distressed soundscape of the moors. We walk up the stake road to get onto the ridge. The stones echo our own steps back to us. Harmony is matching my step to yours. Harmony is noting all the different levels of gold and grey that make up this landscape as the day subsides to the west and the sheep race each other down the field to the feeding trough.

Addleborough Icons: offering themselves as stern though gentle companions for the journey. The landscape divides itself into bands of colour, shaved bark, hammered pewter, golden lichen. Beyond the icons a crescendo of light; beyond that, the dark of Addleborough rising. We walk, for there always is a journey, but we fail to account for how many steps make a distance. Remembering muddles my capacities. Mind but no matter.

When I look again, the icons are still there, staring impassively out of the hills.

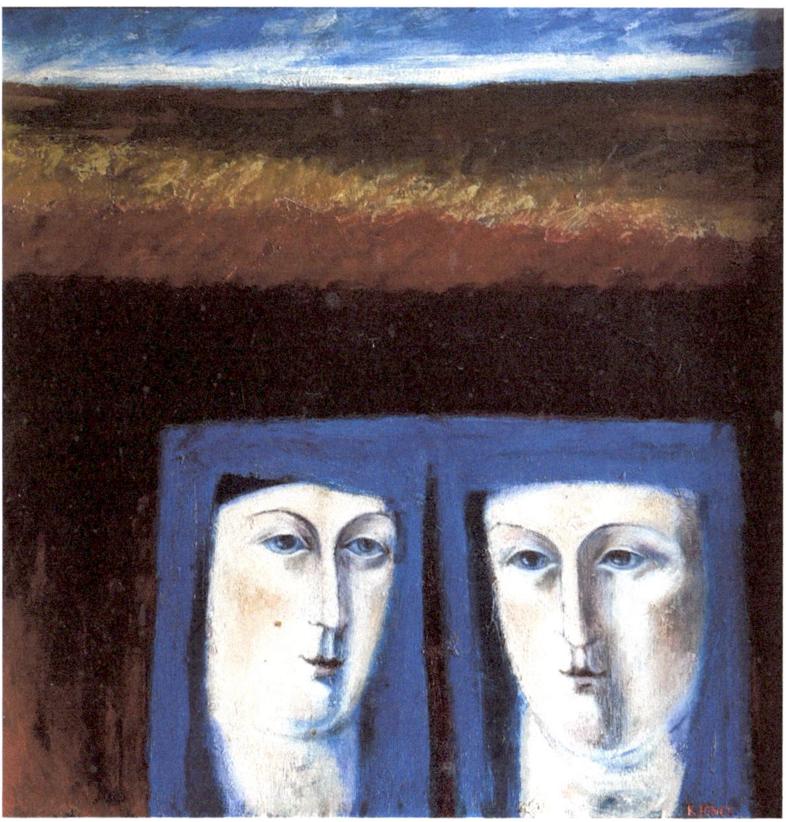

The intersection of things is where we understand them most clearly: a river and a landscape, for example; a body and the earth. Without context, relationship, anything is merely decoration; we cannot access its essential thisness. Yet the understanding is fleeting: a moment of stillness and clarity before the intersection catapults us into the next insight. We are bidden to live in the here and now. Any other time – the future, the past – is banked, well, elsewhere. We might allude to the future or the past, long for them even, but they are interrupted time, almost unreal. What we see clearly in this moment, is now, and shall be forever, and then it is changed, forever, and even thinking of it cannot bring it back.

We took the road up above Dent, a zigzag road, typical of the dale, but don't mistake it for something simple. Here is a series of journeys scratched into stone, sewn into the moorlands. The sun is a roughly cut linen disc in a hessian sky, a slip of white on curdled cream. The climb is brawny, but mesmerising; each step sets something shimmering around the heart. Grisedale and Mallerstang are across to our left; Deepdale and Oughtershaw on our right. The shadows of the clouds race across the fields. The weather curls around us and whips us along. We are not at liberty to resist this. A buzzard lifts off a fencepost, losing a tailfeather. Her flight gives us an intimation of the distances ahead of us before we might reach home.

To write about elemental things: the soil of your land that you mixed with your paint; a jam jar of water from Lake Semerwater; handmade nails hammered into shape and placed just so, to mark a contour – set firm, as if against a gale. A piece of hessian, stretched and soiled and set in place against the spine of the painting. We walk without moving, as you take me under the ridge and out towards Marsett. We weave through the dark, step into the light. The space spinning below us takes our breath away.

If I am quiet enough; if I wish for it hard enough, any moment now you will step out of the studio door and catch my eye.

The studio was always cold, edgy with work, with the smell of white spirit, thinners, turps, oil paint. Behind that, the smell of canvas, wood, stone, the skulls and bones of sheep, rabbits, foxes, birds. See how a crow's beak turns white after death. The jars and tins of brushes, shining in the light, the palette full of urgent mixes. On the walls and on the easels, problems to be solved. Things were rarely going well. Sometimes though, you would talk about the work with excitement, the thrill of uncertainty as you stepped into its impossible perspective, a line that might indicate a hill, under a block that might be the unsettled sky, and all of it lit by a line of red along the horizon.

There is something interesting to be said for everything around us, you told me, and when I look at the work now, I see it crammed with detail – everyday objects in states of repurposed obsolescence: string; tin lids; old fuse boxes become dense with significance, arranged to reveal something arresting and mysterious. In the work, there is nothing trivial or abject, nothing that cannot be redeemed. Everything happens between the astonishing and the mundane, the sacred and the jettisoned, the broken and the recouped, and transforms the common land into something rare. Here is a landscape that is both home and destination, history and endless present. Here is the place where you are brought finally to rest, located peacefully in the restless space of the imagination. Like the land, the work is a palimpsest, elements that are painted over or out remain there, vestigial, humming just under the surface.

I drive here through the cold, snow on the hills and verges, road signs blinded beneath the cataract of sleet. The motorway slewed with black ice. The landscape sits always ahead of me, its old bones shaking. The dark patches of granite or millstone grit look like silhouettes, the earth's cheekbones grazed in the wind. Like the white painting, these whites are breath-white; bone-yellow; black-white; grey. The palette is austere: not condemnatory, but subdued. When I get home, on the turn of the stair, there is the *repoussé* face you made in bronze; if I turn too fast I'll miss the arc of a brow, the empty lozenge of an eye. Steadying myself down for arrival, I pause beside him, and consider myself lucky, given how much he welcomes me home.

Already it is almost February; a rogue sun lowers itself in golden ladders from a grey shelf of cloud to the right of the motorway. In Yorkshire all the roads are broken with bowls of cracked ice. The sky is a piece of beaten tin with a hole roughly cut into it. Gritters salt the length of England. I scramble together some elements to bring back with me – a twist of kindling wood, a square of hessian, a page from a notebook, as if part of letting you go is bringing you with me.

I am moved to consider all the faces you have made or brought to this house, from the Saxon burial stone with its downturned mouth, through to Harlequin dancing, a verdigris copper mask you worked from the back, tiny enamel faces hidden in the crevices. Here is the wooden man made from scraps of wood from your workshop floor; here is the tripartite icon, rendered in watercolour.

Rupture and repair: I salvaged the things you had already lifted from obscurity: a paint tube, flattened and opened – titanium white: *Bianco de Titanio*; a scrap from your notebook, burnt along one perforated edge; and some notes on the work.

'The paintings are to be experienced rather than understood. They do not represent a concealed intention.'

I remember your perplexity on being asked what the paintings were about. The paintings were about the materials used and the process of using them. The shape of a moon, or a rotting apple maybe, in the colours of rust and petrol blue and honey, set into a series of geometries, textures, marks and scratches, describing relatively simple universal forms. The palette is blue-white, like the snow in the woods, like frozen breath, and earth colours, like the bolt on the barn door.

At Busk House, you liked to work in solitude, in the studio that welcomed the western light straight off the slant of the hills. The room was stacked with work, and oddments. Here was the place where crimson lake met phthalo blue to become an apparent black, against which shone hammered bars of copper or tin. Looking trains the eye, you said, and I squinted at the painting because I misheard you and thought you had said: looking trains in the eye. Everything comes down to the way of seeing. Grains of copper dust were swimming in the air, settling on the easel ledges, settling on the wooden benches. At Blades, when you left, there were four small paintings on the stone shelf of the studio, variously unfinished. Each one a question still to be answered; each one a problem to be solved; each one accumulating miraculous bits and pieces to account for a very private way of seeing.

There is a photograph of you in your studio. Your focus is withdrawn from us, attentive to a world that is unaware of the camera. The air around you seems stilled, like held breath. The real presence in this space is the work, the place where ideas and materials coincide, thought and form, spirit and body. Sometimes I feel more and more removed from that way of being in the world, but, marvellously, art invites me back in. Life is full of prodigious complexity, and it distracts us, seduces us down rabbit holes of busyness and frenzy. But art – this singular thing you are creating, in this moment, on this canvas – admits me into a world that is eternal, where I might meet you again and see things your way.

Cruciform landscape I: The depth of the incision in stone. Pale sky stapled to the hills. God's work, an invisible line from heaven to earth; man's work, a red road. In this landscape we might encounter sensation: songbirds, light, the smell of granite under rain. Here we might encounter time: in the guise of history, weather, the self, growing older. The sky is a boulder. The fields waterlogged with rain. There is an invincible welcome for me that rises up in this landscape. No matter where else I am, this is where I belong.

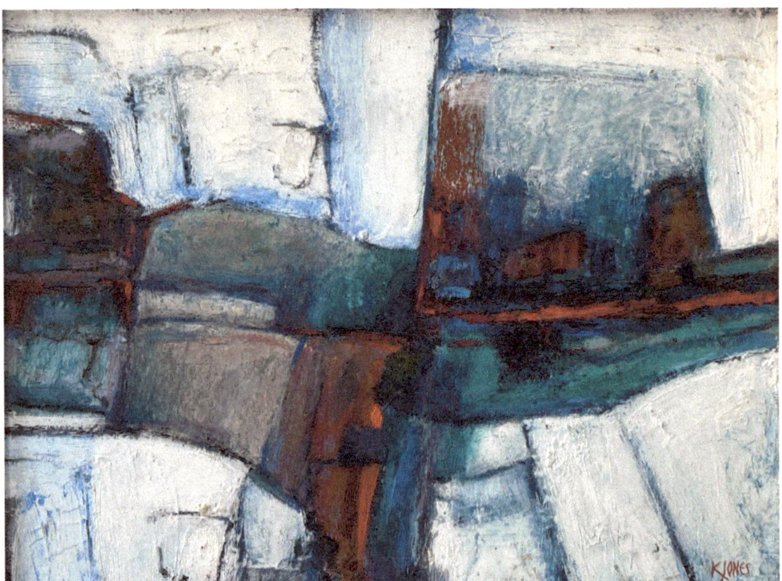

Where there are nettles, the soil is good. In May, when the blackthorn is in bloom, these hedgerows will look like a wedding. In October, they will look like a funeral – the colour of marigolds, and wet wood. I try to get a glimpse of the sky through the hospital window and imagine you did too. It is a sky the colour of milk, with a little blood in it. There is a lump, deep by my rib, in my left breast. I think it might be my heart, but it's too little to be a heart. I negotiate various curtains and couches and doors and all the time experience the longing to be on the moors or in the woods, collecting crow feathers. I strain to hear if there are birds singing. I cannot hear a single thing, but I get the vivid notion that the purple crocuses are opening under the apple tree. It's very small, the doctor says. It's as if you have pushed a dried pea in there. She is trying to reassure me. Except, I haven't, I tell her. And there is no answer to that.

Standing or sitting in the presence of your paintings is as close as I get to expanding time to the point where I might almost be present with you. I am not interested in meaning, then, but in feeling; in experiencing the thing that you have made, in entering into that original, invincible space of feeling. I am aware of my body paying attention, my eyes roving over the surface to find the place where they will settle. The rhythms of the work eventually synching with the rhythms of my body. Then, whatever else is occurring – thoughts, impressions, gulps, heartbeats – I am comforted to be in your company.

A chance as slender as a needle placed vertically in a carpet. The thought that you are still here, standing quiet and intent, just out of my line of sight, painting. You are not exactly withdrawn in this idea. Just focused on discovering something out of reach of what you know already. You lay a layer of chrome yellow over white, over black. It is impossible not to look at this yellow, although, having looked, I have to look away, to see the ghostly burnout of it on my retina; it is like the lances of light that pierce a storm cloud. I want to turn and face you, to ask you… and then I recall that this is just a thought, and the feeling that you are not here is as sickening as treading barefoot with my full weight onto that hidden needle.

The work is so various, experiments and trials clutter the drawers. Drawings, copper-work, notes, letterings. I lift out a small block of wood, the basis for a test engraving. I dust it with a swipe of my thumb, erasing perhaps the dust of your presence, stroking my thumbprint over yours. Engrave, from the middle English *ingrieven*; the word is strikingly close to grave and grief.

I remember, or perhaps imagine, your steady hand, intent on the angle; note your focus, concentrated onto this piece of copper set into black pitch. A letter, a word, an image follows the chisel to arrive on the surface: the letters TA, a tiny brick wall, an arc, a scroll. When I step out into the light, leaves from the Russian vine have been printed by the rain and the wind on the tarmac surface of the drive. I turn the small engraving over in my palm, knowing what a gift it is, how sweetly it fits my grasp.

Peace: Rest in peace we pray over the dead. But I wonder if peace is not rather an active thing. It comes not from absence but from presence. If I take the time to look at the work, really look, not just glance gratefully at the paintings as I pass by, then I feel in the presence of peace. There is something going on. It is quite different from rest, although it has a sort of refreshment to it. The peace that comes from looking at the work is like the peace that comes from doing the work, in that it is absorbing and transforming. I wonder if that is what it is like to be dead, to be endlessly, eternally absorbed and transformed, in peace.

This endeavour to discover you, like raking over the ashes of a fire to discover one ember, has its moments. A careful smashing of your peace, in which you should be allowed to rest – in order to unearth you again.

Very rarely, I catch you in the corner of my eye, and my heart jolts until the vision straightens itself out and I see it is not you, that I must reinvent you for myself. This is not something that happens just because I long for it. If wishing could make it so, I would never miss you. On the occasions when you do appear, you enter under the cover of light, sudden and glorious, dispelling the dark under the bridge between here and there. When you leave, the painting on the wall, that shone too bright to look at, is visible again. The shadow where you might have been has vanished. Everything is as it was.

Through the window, the garden is unfolding its wet green heart, clusters of crocuses under a tangle of apple tree branches; the dark stems of waterlogged roses sulk under a dull sky. The small flamingo willow is wearing its hooped underskirt of red branches. Blackbirds and finches are busy looping in and out. Pigeons conduct their complex mathematics in the trees. Three minus one plus two. Their wings, as they subtract themselves, sound like riotous applause.

And now there is this matter of language, your mind's lexicon disappearing into lacunae. The spaces between things, not the things themselves. I remember you encouraging me to draw that way. To look at what was between the branches of a tree, in order not to draw what I imagined I could see. Now, the uneven light in your eye signals the equivalent of those spaces, as your mind puzzles over what it cannot find to articulate. We address this by walking. In the chinks of the drystone wall, you show me a perfect hemisphere of metal, a clue to someone being there, which you take back to the studio and pierce. Perhaps it will make its way into a painting. The earth has done the work for you, minerals and salts painting the metal into something glorious, as friable as earth and as powerful as salvation. Above us and below us, branches fork and meet the way fiction and fact collide and diverge. When it comes to language, you say, it's the things it can't say that we must pay attention to.

I try and pay attention to them, the sounds that are the things that language cannot say. They are nameless and unspeakable and yet, they mark the days ahead in indelible ways. Sometimes I'm right, sometimes I'm righter, you said. Although the spelling might be off. I don't remember things, you tell people, cheerfully. And it makes me wonder about all the cocked-up continuities of memory, that we take for granted as stable, and refuse the idea that they are provisional and partial. Of course, we pay lip service to it, while we still have the language; we know that our memories conflict with regard to the detail, but, deep down, we feel the rightness of our own. Now yours has receded to the place beyond the pale. And no matter how much we long for it, and try to jog it, no matter how we call it, we cannot retrieve it.

Circles within circles, riddles of colour, how they change in communion with each other. There is a pillar of smoke like a wash of salt against the vanishing act of the black horizon. *Icarus Descending II:* Anything can happen: a boy can fall in a cloud of burning feathers; a man can balance on the soles of his feet in an earthquake, while all around him everything collapses, appalled by his deft capacity for uprightness. Note how the clouds darken at noon in advance of the night. Note the smell of singe. Around that black sun is a line of burnt gold. At the edge of this painting something is unravelling and I don't know what it is.

I wonder if at the end what you remembered best, and in uncomplicated ways, was the garden? The opulent blue of the lawn at daybreak, the canes for sweet peas strung with green twine, the stone shelves for saxifrages and aubretia.

We, whose names and relationships to you you cannot precisely recall, though our identities in love are indistinguishable, move through the rooms of the house. You catch sight of us, or we catch sight of you. Recognition is like that these days. All our other lives, with all their other gardens, flit across this one, like sliding doors, different seasons all held in the lens of the current one, like a compost-heap of lives, settling, being turned, enriching. There are bees in the lupins, a summer's dawn, fresh peas for the shelling, a clutch of rosehips in the snow. I imagine you turning them all over in your mind, allowing the air to reach them. The garden – let's call it life: a place where you could see everything as a delightful surprise or a task still to be completed.

In the graveyard where you are buried, the air is never still. What's left of us, it seems to intimate, is not nothing, but traces, vestiges, elements. It is only possible to enter the cemetery at an angle. The hill is so steep, it feels like staggering. Sheep eat their placid way around the graves. When I am done, though I hate to leave, I ascend the hill, at the speed of my own thoughts; to my right, the Falls are crashing over stones and the sound takes my arm like a faithful relative and leads me home.

What was it like being close to death after all that dying? Did the paintings you never got to paint, paint themselves in invincible perfection? Were you finally pleased with the work? Did the gates of flake white swing back for you to enter your eternal glory? Was the vista fields of gold and lavender and phthalo blue? Was there jazz playing and did you dance? Were there cliffs of back-lit cloud? Did it feel light? Did you know, at last, who we all were and how we loved you and you loved us? Was it just like that?

I might have spoken aloud. I walk against the slope of the empty fell, which of course is not empty but crammed with life and history. Old coins; flints; rusting bolts; baler twine; shrew skulls; beetles; leaf mould; roots; the dead. It takes some grit, actually, to inhabit a life. I might have confided in you, trying to work out my own thoughts. Or perhaps I recited what I could of Yeats, fragments of Blake, of Hughes. Water gushes down the hill; the wind blinds me..

I hold to the hill, under a simmering sky: oyster grey; eggshell; lichen. Orpiment, antique gold, chrome orange, all the colours of natural sunlight sinking into the dark hillside. In the east it is a holy colour. In the west we cannot find anything to rhyme with it. The earth's lines break and then realign. How to get that provisionality into a painting where everything is fixed? Whole fields of colour: storm, scarlet, shark, chalk. The sky takes itself down another register, until it is the colour of dead rabbit under rain. Very soon all this will be swallowed by the night and then it will have to reinvent itself again.

When I think back to The Gables, it is to a childhood time of dens and dark hiding places: looking out from under tables fringed with green velvet tablecloths, or through rhododendron leaves, at a fraught but exciting world, a world duplicated by its shadows, and arguments. It was a time of attics and cellars, each terrifying and compelling in different ways. It was a time of two-storey barns which were dangerous to explore, and old stone outhouses with dead and rotting mangles, covered with ivy. I remember wringing heavy, sodden sheets through that mangle. When I try and describe it now, I find I do not have the vocabulary. Somewhere in my head, the words must be there but they are too heavy to lift, and with them, winding through them, are the things I don't want to squeeze out, yet, like anguish. And maybe memory.

Sounds of childhood: The hiss of a gas fire; daffodil breaking out of its onionskin shell; tea leaves settling in a fortune cup; the bus conductor's ticket machine ratcheting out our tickets; the sound of Jack Narey's horse and cart pulling up Skipton Road. I don't know why one thing seems important while another seems irrelevant. I don't know why memory selects these trivial things to recall that now seem pitifully small to recreate a life. I wonder if that is how it was for you when memory ceased to be faithful – just an ever-diminishing collection of small details. And it makes me think of the paintings: a flattened bottle top, a piece of slate scored with a stone, the shine of something unrecognisable in the dark.

In the dark, the shape of a barn differentiating itself, and headlights moving across the opposite wall of the valley. And the dark is so alive with presence, sensation, otherness. It is like being inside a painting. When I emerge from it, I discover again how much I like the way you lay the flake white down, next to that almost disappearing line of charcoal fire.

The purple and white hellebores under the shade of the grey wall: according to Hippocrates, a cure for mental illness. The white anemone in the wood: a symbol of healing and a sign of death. The kingcup in the field, held under a chin: signifying a childhood love of things that would not melt. In the garden, the blooms of adoration: love in the mist; lad's love; love-lies-bleeding, bleeding hearts. You never came in from the garden without flowers, a small handful for the house. When you died the house was full of them, to lift the mood of suffering. I could not look at them; their lines were imprecise, blurred. All I could think was that once they had been living.

What is heavier, body or earth? It was hard to carry you down the hill from the church to the grave. We were unbalanced, or maybe it was just me who was unbalanced. The wind whipped my hair into my eyes. There was an odd, vertiginous rake to the path because of the weight of you; it seemed to want to tip me over. All the lines were unsettled or uneven. Even the word grief failed to make sense, quite distanced from what we were experiencing. We laid you in the narrow cupboard of the earth. Impossible.

Just as impossible as it is to consider how the world feels now that you are gone. What happens when the giants of our lives die and we are left to mill around, have our small ideas, press on through every kind of weather, all of us utterly capsized by what has occurred?

Local weather gushes down the windows. The rain has sucked up the land, rattling the cinder path by the back door, skimming the flags with wet and soot; the wind has blown the garden leaves into eddies and spirals. I am looking through your sketchbooks, all the concentric circles, spirals, arcs, the endless curved journeys of our lives. In the workshop, spirals of wood-shavings, swarf, copper are carefully gathered because you can see the lesson there. Your studio at Busk was up a spiral staircase: to reach the places where we might create, we cover the ground we have covered before, only higher up. The learning is both repetitious and progressive.

The studio: a waiting room: the work before the work is properly begun. A rough patch of paint on a canvas, suggesting perspective; a rectangle, terracotta or grey, an arc, maybe made by a brush, or a stick; maybe made by pressing a piece of something into the wet paint, there to be imagined but not yet in play. Blocks of thought, waiting for you to take up the brush again. A sketch book open, shapes on the page made up in equal measure of lines and thoughts; shapes and *aides-mémoire* of walks or other ways of noticing. Here, where I am deeply aware of endings, are numerous beginnings, each one starting to say something different. They surface as provocations, an intimation of what you had to say, lost in the midst of all that now must remain unsaid.

There are forms, gathered in the treetops, that you take to be angels. They are angels in black feathers with blue-black tips. They hover on the border between familiar and phenomenal. Their song, which is like enough to birdsong, makes a three-dimensional aural account of the landscape. Shadows move over your grey eyes. As always, you can see things I might miss: the colours in the compost-heap, composing and decomposing themselves; a wren's nest, blown out of its safe harbour and under the table where we are eating a lunch of cheese and apples; the shape of a fish moving over the river stones.

You scarcely signed your work. Sometimes your two initials crossing each other in red paint, sometimes your full surname, sometimes just a pencilled note on the reverse. Now, when I search for these marks that signal who you were and what you did, it strikes me how scant they are, how prescient of what we did not know, and how much we would miss. Instead of a signature, a chalice. In lieu of your name, you, before the easel, painting a blue stripe across the bottom of the canvas, gesturing towards what it could bear, knowing exactly what it could not.

Painting doesn't depend on memory – or only in the way that muscle memory allows you to make the line just there – but when it was made, you weren't remembering. You were looking for the one invisible, real thing that you could bring into visibility. In *Cornwall III* there are three pale blue dots on a white wall, like three blue moons on a silver dish, so small and startling it is hard to believe they are there. They are a blue I haven't seen much, shimmering in the infinite present of the world of the painting.

For drawing, you always favoured a 6B pencil, soft and black. In the bottom right-hand corner of this painting is your signature, in exactly that.

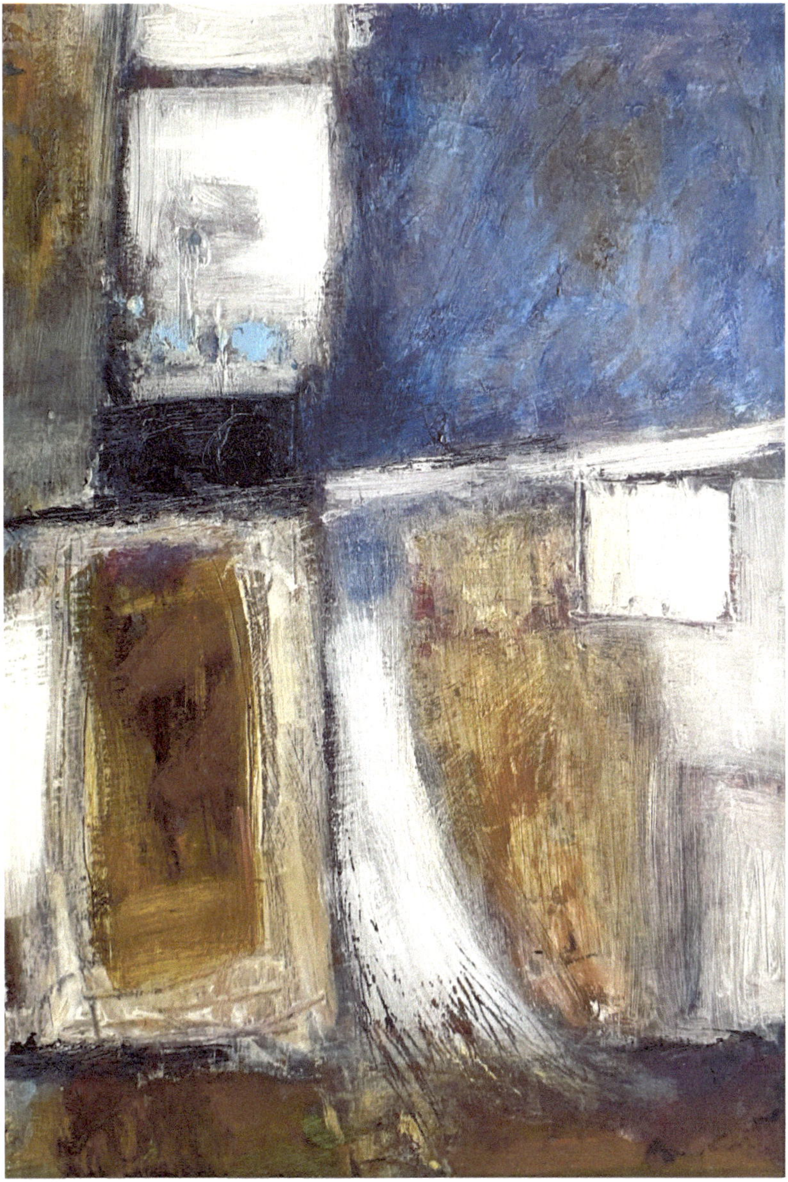

Just as a window implies an inside and an outside, the frame suggests to us where we should pay attention. It directs our gaze, yet inside the frame the space opens up; we wander across the planes and landscapes. A small passage of black, scratched and scuffed, snags our vision. It seemed black, but now its blackness shines with blue, like a mussel shell or a puddle of stagnant water outside the abattoir. Beyond this, shadows and minerals: bronze, zinc, copper, tin, scabs on leaves, ashes and clinkers from the grate. Each thing is tender and bright, shining. Each thing making its sound, differentiating itself from what surrounds it.

I went into a gallery to look at the things artists had made. They were interesting, but so were the walls. The walls were just as interesting, a palimpsest of the room's other histories: two perfect circles of 1930s pink, where pipes had been stoppered by plaster or filler; scour marks where a chisel had passed; lines where copper pipes had not been painted over; the oblongs and squares of Payne's grey, which had once been the backing for electrical sockets; scuffs; putty; the marks left by old tape; brickwork and pencil marks. It was as good as art in expressing what defies language.

Yellow: a revelation in lichen, the heart of a buttercup, slightly sour jelly sweets, the thirteenth letter of the alphabet, mellow. Yellow: a sprint along the beach to find a twist of nylon rope, soft moth at a window, a goat's eye, dirty. Yellow: Malvolio's hose, a garden hose, winter jasmine against a bitter blue sky, inviolable. Yellow: double lines, no parking, Belisha beacons, the handles of the scissors in the house of blades, bold. The shimmering surface of gold leaf, *Gloire de Dijon* roses, the buffed reverse of a paint tube, cadmium yellow, courageous. It was one of the first words I learned to read. Yellow? you query, with a twinkle in your grey eyes. It's never been yellow. It's crushed canary.

Green: the bloom on a mouldy orange, an old bruise, water left too long in the sunlight, troubling. Green: the sky before the storm breaks, emeralds swapped for balloons, the North Sea in Whitby, new leaves on the willow, precise. Green: the eyes of a black cat, a herb garden, a bowl of fresh limes, astute. Green: the shine on a bay tree when the sun finds it, gorgeous, the word sticks in my mouth, though I like the zh in the middle. Green: the high hum of a child's spinning top. Grass: the scent of summer.

There is a painting you did that sections the sky between thin telegraph poles. They make it look as though the sky is roughly stapled into place. What do telegraph poles do? They allow us to speak across time and space. The walls there are blue-grey, grey-green. The fields are as green as the sound of church bells. But something about here recalls whatever you saw there, or else, whatever I saw in that painting.

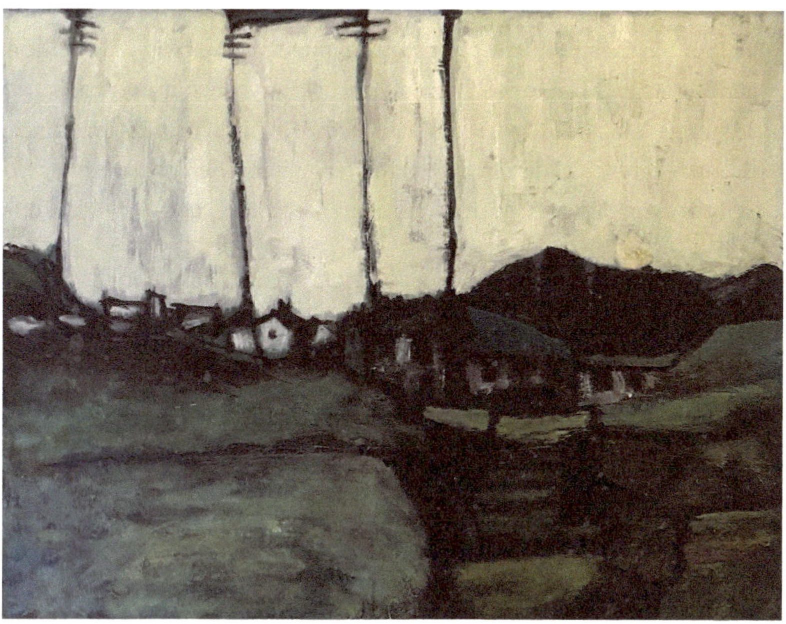

There was a kitchen, with a Rayburn in it, where we lived most winters; the rest of the house froze frost ferns on the window. We took candles to light us to bed. There was always a chopper hanging on the wall, ready to fulfil its part of the bargain. As well as the axe, dried herbs in bunches, charms and tokens cluttered our dreams. When we are living in the present, we never imagine it will become a past we will look back on. I never saw you lick a pencil; you always opened your knife and shaved flakes of wood and graphite into sharpness. The pleasure of making a line with that freshly sharpened pencil was like flying a kite; I could hardly believe it, but there it was. By the time you tipped the shavings into the Rayburn, I had already taken the edge off it.

Our toys were home-made, repurposed from the stuff of someone else's life into the theatre of our play: glove puppets with *papier-mâché* heads; painting wheels fashioned from old record players; stilts; go-carts from old prams; magic lantern boxes; dark rooms; kilns; lino cuts for printing our own cards; a slide made from a stepladder. There was nothing you could not do. Flakes of burnish fell from your hands that were blackened with work.

Strips of me flying in the wind. The zipwire you made us from the tree house to the pear tree, the handles of an old scooter all we had to hang onto as we dropped through the air into terror-shot-joy, our breath just behind us.

What was there before painting? A collection of materials, things on which and with which to make a mark. What comes between the stuff and the mark? A decision. No painting can be made without a decision. What comes after painting: the fire, the kiln, incisions in metal. What comes between the painting and the fire? A decision. You decide what to jettison and what to keep. What did you decide? I forget. What comes after forgetting? Looking. No painting can be made without looking. I think of you now, standing before the easel, peering into it, all the stuff of decision-making at hand. What came next? I forget.

In the workshop: hammers and saws; tins of screws, nails, washers, bolts, each tin meticulously labelled. The old bench, notched and worn. The vice clamped to it, waiting to be used. Chisels, bradawls, spirit levels, measuring tapes, tins with stubs of pencils. Nothing rusty to be found, though that is what I am hoping for.

In the studio: tins of brushes in the eggshell-coloured light, the smell of white spirit, metal drawers full of paints; skulls, sketchbooks, easels. A lintel of stone and low sun. Rags.

On the stone windowsill: a light facsimile of the window – the reverse of a shadow. Pieces of rusted metal. Here they are, of course. A dead fly. On the other side of the window, all the different grasses of the field, rock hard flinty rain, a couple of months until another Christmas without you.

Missing you feels like a very distinct kind of aloneness – not that there aren't people around me who love me, but that you, who loved me in the very particular way you did, have withdrawn. The world is full of things that recall you, but they recall you with a pang. I try to remind myself that there is always more presence than absence, even if that presence seems itself to be waiting for your engagement with it. What was it Louis MacNeice said? Something along the lines of the world being suddener and more various than we imagine. Something like that. World is crazier. Perhaps it is enough to recognise the variousness, and that in your paintings your actions exist in the world, and all of the paintings invite me to draw close to you, each in a specific and unique way. There is no doubt that the world is fuller and more alive because of you. The more I look, the more I feel like the distance between us shifts.

I cannot tell if these thoughts are protections or obstacles. There are days I take some comfort from them, sensitive to the notes of lament around words like stone and remnant, mask, line and copper glaze. These are the six words that come around again and again. I crouch at the back of the garden, waiting to see if something random and new might arise from their repetitions, as if longing itself could summon you up, were evidence of some sort of quantum entanglement. The thing about entanglement is that we are all entangled. We are not separate, however much we might appear to be. The stone is intimately linked to me. Bishop Berkeley, the eighteenth-century Irish philosopher, argued that everything we perceived was an idea. Samuel Johnson kicked a stone, saying: *Thus do I refute him*. The stone, though, is the idea, and it is part of the idea of me too. Each remnant connects me to the painting and to you, and the mask shifts, the line breaks and then reassembles itself for the moment when I perceive it. Copper-glazed. It's almost like heaven.

The thing I am paying attention to here is a metal disc, picked up from the street: it is blue, the blue of spat-out toothpaste, budgie blue. If I squint at it, at a certain tilt, I can make out a pencil line, disappearing, like the ghost of a bird on glass.

If I squint even more narrowly, it becomes a blue moon, cratered, rough. Perhaps there is a face there. Moon-face disc – so different from the ones you enamelled, and yet inscrutably connected to them. When I stop squinting and turn this disc over in my hand, it could be the gift from a man, standing in a fire, watching it turn from molten to blue in the cooling light.

Imagine an old penny, one of the large ones, hammered thin and irregular. Imagine it scored with little marks, like filings or accountings, or the markings of rain on a gloomy window. I keep trying to return to you via the work, or to return you to me. It's frustrating, because it gets me nowhere, yet it does also seem to take me somewhere. I cannot bear to be indoors, so I go into the garden with its glint of coming rain. Xantippe sends me a video of Brighton Pier where the starlings are moving like iron filings, making the sign for infinity in the sky, and, out of nowhere, a sun the size and shape and texture of the beaten copper penny, enamelled into rose gold, briefly obliterates everything I can bear to look at.

What doesn't stick falls, and keeps on falling. What does art do? It takes us to where we are not known, where we might clasp ourselves to the unfamiliar, step out of or into our pasts. In the dale, a road composed of bleating sheep stops me in my tracks. I slow down for them. They make a sound like shaken tin. The rain comes casting down. What doesn't stick falls, and keeps on falling: the sheep pour themselves through a gap in the wall and into a field. Ruts in the road run with reflected sky. Small rivers burst from the hills and change the lines of what is known. In the gardens of these dales longhouses, rose petals battered by the rain become tea-stained, blown. There is a child but we cannot tell which child it is, for she has her face buried in a rose as big as her head.

Everything in the past is irregular. The first ten years were the years of scuffed knees and sticklebacks and minnows in jam jars down by the canal. They were the years of grey kittens, burning my hair, burning my fingerprints off my fingers, flying down homemade zip wires through the green garden to a man in an overcoat holding an apple in the palm of his hand. The first ten years were the years of rain: wet roads, wet cellars, wet fish-and-chip papers, full wet blooms on the peonies. The rain in italics, perpetually writing its gushing stories and rinsing them away again.

The next ten years were the decade of love: long summers, surrendered virginity, reckless happiness and towering misery. Your face, when you emerged from the studio, which was a lean-to in glass, was steady: you were not present, you were thinking. Or creating. That is, you were present, but you were present elsewhere. Work was happening. The studio was a place where things were either molten, or plunged into cold water or slung into the bin, from which I rescued various now treasured items. On the street side of the house, an ice-cream van failed to kill its engine, squatted at the kerb, endlessly unspooling its nostalgic chimes. Everything winds back into itself. A pink bed full of kittens from the decade before.

The third ten years were the decade of marriage and children. You became a grandfather, able to step into the light of your own beloved grandfather. It was the decade of hand-made toys and home-made bread, a horse's head carved in wood for the rocking horse. It was the decade of the icon paintings.

An arc, a chalice cupping the sometimes light: a brief glance will identify this as the white painting. Further attention reveals not a single white. Two thin charcoal lines form the arc. Against them a colour coaxed from light – hard to identify – the colour of ice breaking over a puddle. Beyond this, boat shapes, in greys, black, blue. Around them the bleached-out colour of peeling paint on Victorian seaside lampposts. Not white, but vanilla ice cream in the rain. Not white, but the pink interior glow of a clamshell; the grey of rain-washed masonry; the colour of chimney smoke rising against a mill-town sky. Not white, more the colour of old chewing gum stamped into unwashed pavements. Not white, but hellebore, mist in the wet field, or a shire horse the colour of rough quartz.

Earth painting, rough-textured, deep. Green shot with blue-black, the colour of beetle-backs, bruise green, labradorite, soot black. Cement, sand, stone, a disc of bright gold, broken. Reflections both figurative and literal. The unstable colours of water, pewter and charcoal. A smell like silver polish rising from the land. The warmth of pure rust, or bracken, flickering in certain lights. And in the bottom right hand corner, your signature: still fiery, but almost extinguished.

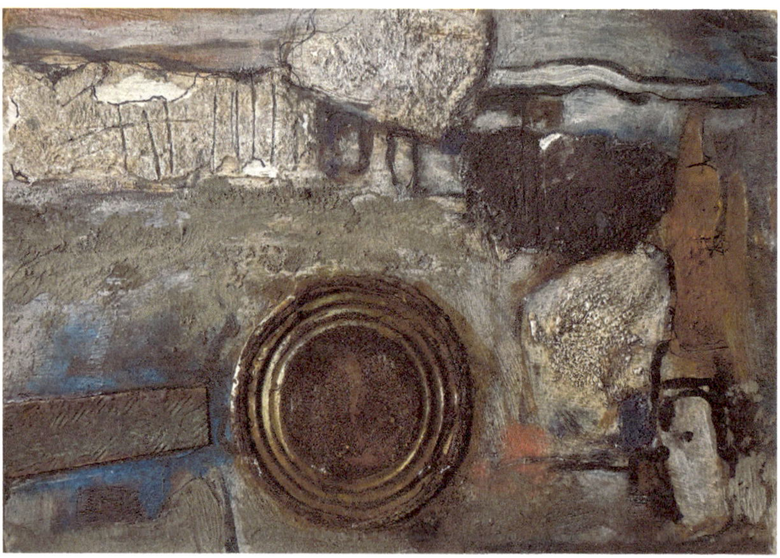

Ineptitude. Not something I associate with you, except later, of course, when the ability to do things got warped by dementia, and then it didn't seem like you at all. It seemed, if anything, illusory – a lapse of judgement, a scrambling of different skills. We couldn't quite believe it – we laughed; a drill into a water-pipe? A mirrored cupboard door hung upside down? A suitcase full of tuna tins, carefully washed and collected. The results suggested a vision of the world that was just as arresting, just as original, just as off-key as anything you had made in the years before. Everything requested our attention, a word that carries with it, as distant relatives, both tension and tenderness.

Reading poetry aloud, for the pleasure of hearing the words forming in the air and filling it. Reading aloud, my first experience of reading. My first read-aloud word: wolf. The story became apocryphal. Later, the majestic poets: Yeats, Blake, Heaney. Very early I learned that the word was the beginning and also the end. You and me walking the line of the hills with these giants who brought the landscape to us in ways that both altered and affirmed it. Or on Sunday afternoons at King's Head, with the fire burning in the grate, and the rain lashing outside; the room holding its breath for the sound of your voice reading to us. Not just us, but every listening child: the boy you were at school, listening to the story of Icarus; the children still to be born who would later curl into the space, an ancestral space, made of the stories you told, and the poems you knew by heart. When I think of this legacy, it seems to me as vast and deep and particular as any of the paintings. And, if I am very still, I can almost hear it again.

There is no need for art to strive to be like everything else. Art isn't about photo-realism. It's about emotion. There are concerns now about AI and how it might supersede artists, or composers, or writers. But I think it won't, and that is partly because of its facility for perfection. Humans strive for perfection (indeed, we make a virtue out of perfectionism), which prevents us actually making art – and I think it prevents computers as well. Because we don't really go to art for perfection. We go to it for redemption. To see our suffering redeemed. AI won't make art, and it can't, because it has never suffered.

I was thinking about how we approach creative work, how we must not bring anything we know to it, but we must approach it naked and vulnerable and step into the mystery of where it leads us. It is no good if we arrive defended before the work. The work is like love or life; it can't save us from ourselves or from each other. All it can do is be true.

And I was wondering if that made it easier for you to make your peace with dementia – all those years of arriving with nothing, but being willing to step into the terrifying and magical unknown to see where the work would lead you. Did that afford you a certain graceful curiosity about what this next stage would be like?

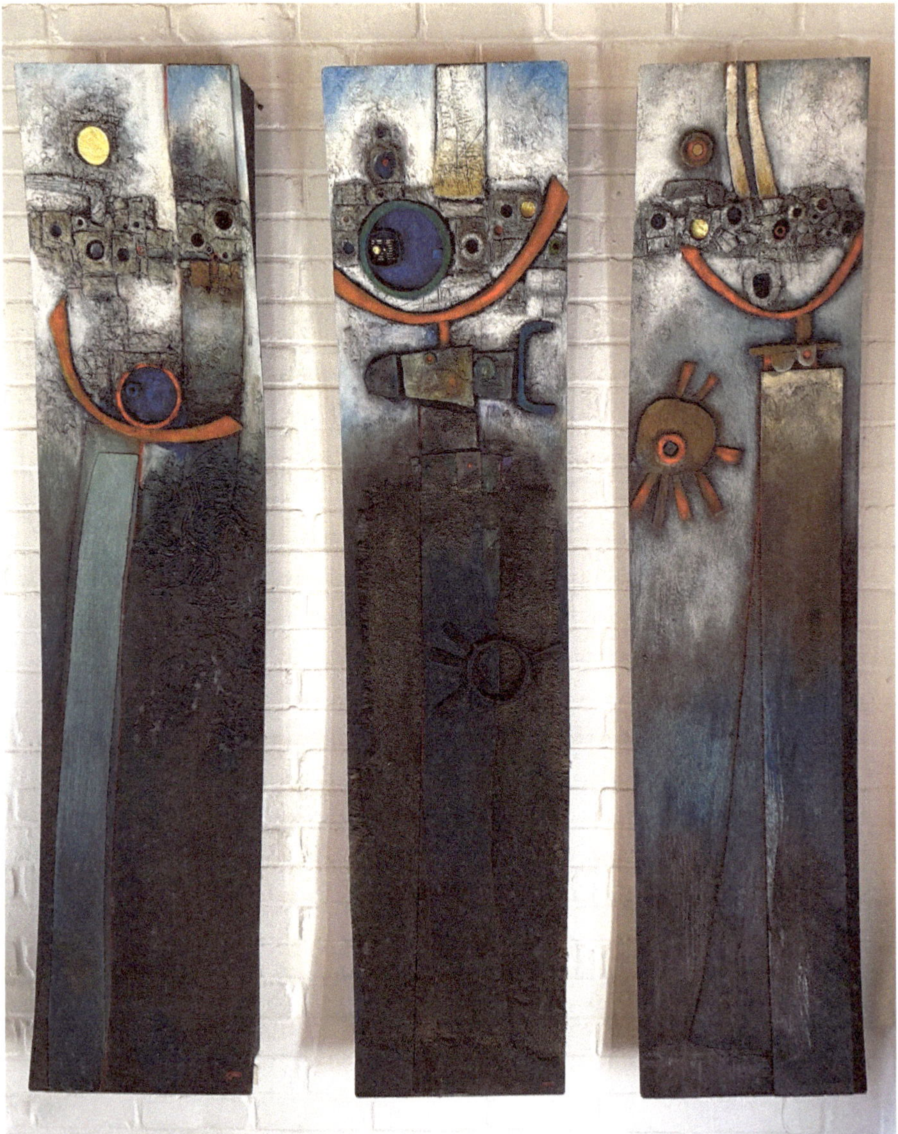

Triptych: three curved panels, massive, heart-stoppingly bold. Here are the paintings it will take me a lifetime to see.
I: a sun flaring. Perhaps it is a comet, or a furnace. A crucible of sooted light. An uneven laddering of layers, paint and wood, forms that catch and hold just at the brink where what might be is nearly, but not quite.
II: an eclipse dropping. That arc might just be angelic wings, blue riding on blue.
III: shards of the cruciform dark. A sun, falling.

The bravura is breath-taking; the jeopardy phenomenal. According to these paintings everything is interesting: wormcasts, walls, hessian, circles, suns and water and soil and shadows. Of course, there is a spiritual dimension to them, they are soaring works, reaching towards radiance, unity, mercy. More than two thirds of each work is devoted to the underworld. Things unfold and then fold back into themselves, suggesting both revelation and mystery. They are rough and tender, huge and fine. They remind me of God because they are so present and yet so beyond me. Remind is not quite the term: they bring God close to my mind, but also, they bring me into His mind, and into yours and that is an astonishingly creative space to be brought into.

What is belief? It is what occurs when certainty that something is not the case doubts itself. Each of these paintings invites us to believe in something, even if we cannot say precisely what it is.

Here is the painting of the bursting dark, smoke yawning through a stone grate, a granite blackness with a flaked edge that strikes a solid note. If the painting were a human – and it is more than six feet tall – where the heart might be is a tiny red square, a millimetre by a millimetre. It is like a red shadow, patched and nailed, and glowing through the body of the work. The dead are dead, a woman tells me. Perhaps so, but you don't seem dead. Perhaps the work of the dead is like the work of the artist – to go deep into the underworld to find out what is there and bring it back. Perhaps the work of the dead is to enter the red square and find the angel crouching there, striking a light between the two flints of this world and the next.

It's like magic; I cannot see how you do it. I look for the marks you make with your hand, with a brush, but the painting comes fully formed, and cannot be deconstructed. I think of Rothko's squares and how he never wanted anyone to know how he got those deep saturations of colour. For him they were unique elements in unique situations: reds and violets over red. Wondrous ideas expressed vividly and exactly to make the viewer feel something they have never felt before. This is exactly how I feel about the works I have; I look at them searching for you and I find instead the startling thing I have never felt before. Each time it is like a pain in my heart and each time it is like a gift.

Don't think twice: if I could catch up with you for a moment, would all our moments be present together? The day you shouted, 'Bring me a balalaika back,' as the train pulled out of the station and I, at fifteen, was on my way to Russia; the day you showed me how to bring a fish out of a piece of wood; the day we stood at the threshold of the church together on my wedding day and you said: you don't have to do this, you know. It took us all a while. A long time. Just the mess of ordinary life. But not long enough in the end. And yet it is these small accumulations of memory that make the things that we remember. I need to slow myself enough to hear my second thought.

As a child, I used to fear the dead, totally sure of the presence of ghosts, presences which felt huge and not always friendly. Now, when I long for it, there is nothing: not the suggestion of presence behind me, not a shiver in the air, not a changing in the quality of light to suggest you are around. I long for you to make yourself known, in the quietest of ways: in dreams, in signs that are painted on trees: visual puns that might just as well be you, but are so patently not you that they leave me feeling how much I miss you, and that missing you is like missing the point – I am incapable of explaining it. Even thinking of you is no more than a tender blur, like finding a photograph, or your writing on a scrap of paper, ephemeral. Almost unbelievable evidence that you did once exist like that. Unlike the paintings, which stand up for you tremendously. Trying to find you is like trying to find a character – there is a sort of mirage between me and the person I am creating – I enter that idea of you, am somehow there, and yet it isn't me, and it isn't exactly you either.

To be honest, the work was everything. I could drive for five hours to arrive at your house and you would not come down from your studio. It made me mad. Even as a child I berated you, telling you that you spent too much time with your painting. It was exacting work, and also, often, fruitless. Now, of course, I am greedy for everything you spent your time with. Time in contemplation of any one of the paintings affords me endless time with you. I wonder if that thought ever crossed your mind. I find you by surprise, maybe in the same way that you found yourself, while lost (and not lost) in the act of painting. As a child, I always felt you were lost to me when you painted. I complained about it. Now, the light will fall upon the canvas in a certain way, and colours that I had not seen previously rise to the surface and shine out. And in the space between looking and seeing, you arrive. Or perhaps it is the painting that arrives, in a wholly new form. Or perhaps it is me, deepened with a shade of you.

I wonder about all the things I must have overlooked, they must be teeming about me, if only I could train my eyes to see them. How blind I must be. Even when I try to look again, I can only see the blunt stuff that everybody sees. If I close my eyes, the sparking shreds of light that dart about on the eyelid's inner surface, remind me not to look at anything directly. Perhaps the reason why we have to look again, is that sometimes things only appear when you are looking just to one side of them. Some things simply cannot be seen straight on.

I thought I knew where I was when you were alive: my constant north. There was a magnetic current that kept me steady. Ideas, discussions, rebellions, jokes, inventions, everything, every word and thought formed part of the whole narrative, or image, of who I imagined I was. Now, none of that text makes any sense at all. The words fail me. And I am minded to consider that it is like both dementia and creativity. I do not see things quite the way I used to; things shake but stay resolutely broken, like the arrow shivering in a compass, trying to find north but failing.

Each year, I return to the garden, to walk the perimeters of honeysuckle and lad's love, to gather roses of deep and old-fashioned sweetness. You could not see the point of an unscented flower. Many's the time you would go out into the rain to bring a single bloom back into the house for Mum. Even the trees are scented: lilac, apple, pear, ceanothus. Each spring, these trees bloom into being, intensified by the rain, by the first strong sunlight of the year. In the borders, if we can call them borders – my garden is too unruly for that to be really accurate – broom and wild mint have grown out of hand; here are artemisia, dianthus, daffodil. It takes my breath away; I never expected anything to feel so immediate.

Easter Day, we hid foil-covered eggs in your silver birch. The woods were blowy, grey-skied, full of crows. The house no longer contained you, and it was hard to look at; its boundaries were blurred by rain. Glints passed quickly over the windowpanes; I could see through them, but fragmentedly, imperfectly. The world seemed more mercurial, dizzying, resurrected – like looking at something through a magnifying lens. It felt almost monstrous, in the ways that dreams feel, beyond words. Utterly mysterious.

I wonder how often in painting you felt at one with yourself, at one with creation. My recollections falter, although more often than not I seem to remember you fighting with it: a painting that couldn't be resolved; enamel that burned out; frames that wouldn't meet. The oneness that you might have felt skittered away from you, left you jittery and angry. The house smelled of hot metal and molten glass. The house smelled of wood-shavings and paint thinners, and the oily, plasticky smell of paint. I treasure the pieces I rescued from your bins and I mourn the ones that I failed to save. Not that everything you did was brilliant – just that all of it now is as precious as rain running off a glass, a daylight moon, a pebble broken open to reveal a quartz heart; not rare exactly, but if we were never to see such a thing again, our lives would be poorer.

Perhaps painting is like language – a kind of fluency that is given if you are lucky, and might be learned if you are not. Fluency – the word itself suggests flow, movement, dynamism. An alertness to mutability and difference. We don't see a painting in a single glance or even a gaze. Our eyes move around over the surface, detecting depths and layers, seeing this passage here in itself, and then as part of the whole. A colour or a brushstroke means one thing in isolation and then another when seen from further back. Emotions rise in us, and possibly also recognition. A note from your notebook: Art takes time, but to look at a painting even for one hour, uninterrupted, is difficult.

Think of it this way, you suggested, a painting is never finished; it is in constant flux, happening again and again, like creation itself. It is always reinventing itself. That's why it is so hard to frame paintings, give them a title, announce them as a complete thought. A painting is more like a conversation than a thought. It can be picked up by anyone and taken off in a new direction.

Sometimes, you said, painting is as much about deletion as it is about addition, scraping the paint back to reveal a new texture, a graze of colour which would be otherwise unachievable. In the National Gallery, you showed me how Rembrandt used the sharpened end of a paintbrush to draw into the paint. Now when I look at your paintings I see that those marks you made that I thought were about erosion are also about plenitude. In my mind's eye, Rembrandt's self-portrait as an old man gives me the ghost of a smile, as though I finally understood something you have been trying to say. And I think again about life, and memory, and art, and how we make things in order to understand them. I'll stop now, and just sit with that thought.

Over the years, we walked a long way, often in the rain, which has a blunting, foreshortening effect on vision. Graphite trees emerged from the clouded landscape, drew close into something three-dimensional, real, textured and sensual. Sometimes, the only evidence of trees in the distance was the sound of the rooks, calling. Every sound had its echo; even our breath added to the soundscape.

The hills are layered with the dead: sheep skulls picked clean by crows; rabbits riddled by the wind and rain; leaves blackening, losing their form. We picked them up sometimes, brought them home like treasure. Not once did it occur to me that you might one day be part of that composition.

Half-way up the slope, the sky streams away from me. Things that seemed stable lurch. A curlew, so high it is invisible, calls and sets the season. Below me is the ruined church; beyond that, the lake. The spirit of God moves across the surface of the water in shadows and ripples: burly, unmissable.

Millions of lives have been lived here, in this complex light, in this earth-music of wind and bird and water. It makes me giddy to think of them, it unbalances me. I heard on the radio that in Australia, people greet their ancestors, tell them they are here. I wonder how far back someone has to have died to become an ancestor. People sink into time, lose themselves in the shadows. The earth gets richer; it hoards us. I sit on the slope of the hillside next to your grave and place my hands upon it, to feel it. Here I am, I say. But it seems indifferent.

Light, the colour of dust, over Addleborough. We drive across the moors towards Richmond in slanting rain, sunshine, brilliance and black cloud. The static blur of land seen through rain on the car window, coded, digital, on-off, on-off. Not analogue like the eye sees. Ruined castles rise, implacable, somehow scaled to the majesty of the land: Castle Bolton; Richmond Castle, dwelling places for ghosts beneath the sky-high gods and angels who look on. The Falls are in full spate. Verges of daffodils shine, rattled in the weather, just a flash of primary colour in the earth-tones. The landscape is stately, a thing we might merely witness, not belong to. And yet I get the distinct impression that if I were to stop the car, and place my ear to the road or the wall or the field, I would hear the low-pitched hum of the land and I would recognise it.

In the graveyard, sheep tend the covers of the dead. Here the light is restrained by the shadow of the church. Here time makes no difference. The walls, fancy with lichen and mosses, demonstrate the day's shine. When I look again, trees are coming into blossom, or into catkin; the motorways are clear of roadworks and diversions; and here you are again, drumming your fingers on the edge of the table, keeping time with love.

The rain shows no sign of stopping as I drive through the dale, pulling myself up winding hills into fiercer weather. Across the valley it falls, soft and dark into the sodden land. A partridge scuttles across the road, like a flash of bracken and blue sky. The road churns downwards, pothole puddles reflecting grey, the windscreen wipers obliterating, clearing, obliterating, clearing. The wing of a rook, dead at the side of the road, flaps weakly as I pass it, bones and feathers. Above Redmire, the sky clears to the colour of old chewing gum and a small rogue sun appears above the ledge of High Harker hill. Streams burst from the bog. Up here, anything is possible, even a change in the weather.

Totemic Structure 1: Mixed media: Consider the painting – if this is a painting – as a thought becoming visible, or perhaps not a thought, but an experience, or even a recognition. Although the recognition might only come in the act of painting. The work is not, I believe, a rendition of a recognition. It is an exploration, a series of questions seriously attended to. And, in that, it might be like faith. Imagine putting a frame around that and saying: there, it is finished. Well, you couldn't frame this. It is not accessible in that way. In order to be finished, it requires the viewer to engage with it. Have a completely new thought. The thought – or the work – trembles, reasserts itself, rearticulates itself according to the light. When I look at your paintings now, I see something impossible to see in the morning. When the light catches them in a certain way, the colours that are hidden appear on the surface like a revelation, or an epiphany.

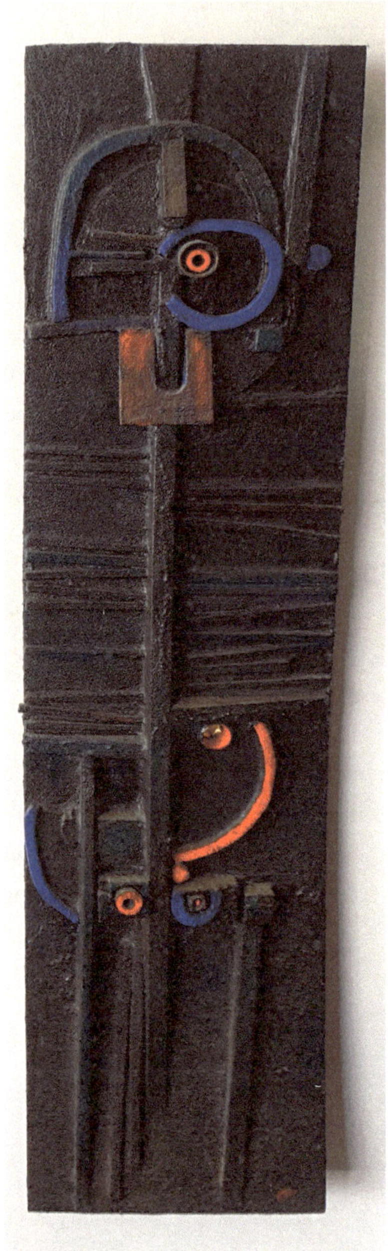

Woodworker: necessary tools: a good eye, sensitive hands, patience. The secret of working with wood is to understand that it was once alive, that it felt the rain, the wind moving through its branches and leaves, that it felt the quality of the soil which was the sustenance for its roots. Sometimes shakes arise in the wood, small fissures or stresses. Falling, or being felled, can do that to a tree.

Painter: necessary tools: a good eye, a steady hand, a willingness to explore a landscape of feeling through the sudden energies of colour. Veils of paint poured from ladders at ceiling height; marks made with stones, or pieces of wood, or a brush. Sometimes, the weather is so dark that all it needs to shake it into brilliance is a small lemon-coloured rectangle exactly placed.

Enameller: necessary tools: a steady hand, fire, glass, smoke and water. The world retreats not knowing what it wants. All there is is the mouth of the kiln and a hand offering art to the flames. Inside the kiln, forms collapse into a glowing shadow, make their connection to something miraculous. There is a tiny, charred window into this molten world. Rain hurls itself at the studio door, roaring to be allowed in.

Artist: necessary tools: vision, determination, insight, honesty, curiosity. Potentially a sense of humility, or perhaps humbleness is more onomatopoeic. You strap your heart to the mettle and make it work for you. Something stronger than rain batters at the door. A throng of ideas to get down, quickly. Something pure and strong: limpid as cooling glass in the rain, radiant as a magpie leaping from a tree. Into the plum-dark thunder you bring a lozenge of cadmium chartreuse. The synonym for lemon, you tell me, is failure. It's not true, of course; we both know that the synonym for lemon is a black cat.

A failure. Nevertheless, I retrieve your failures from the bin and treasure them. I marvel at what you could be failing to see in them. I hold them up to the light and they disappear into the dark. I hold them up to the paintings that are not failures, and there is an unerasable intimacy between one image and the next. Behind me, on the table, is a pewter bowl with a lemon in it. I think about the things you save: old metal, tuna tins, seedheads, offcuts; and I think about the things you jettison: failed work, more failed work, ideas. Is it worth the emptiness that follows? I want to ask.

I want to ask about a series of collapsing circles. What makes them work in this painting? How did you know? I offer them my deep regard. How tender they are. They emerge and recede, just on the periphery, the perimeter, of my field of vision. I wonder why it is called a field and not, say a window or a jungle. The window of vision frames an opportunity to see things differently; the jungle of vision is the closest we might come to the messy accuracy of the unknown. The words radiate outwards from the centre, rain on the surface of the lake. Draw me a circle, Dad, I say, and you carefully draw a straight line and smile at me. I can't tell whether you know or don't know.

What type of tree is this? I ask, near the silver birch, hoping to find the thing you will remember easily. These are cypresses, you tell me, the most popular tree in Persian gardens. They symbolise eternal life. Like the circle.

Like the circle, a moon in a daylight sky appears to empty itself. It defies looking, even when I look again. A cloud passes over it and it is like the lobe of God's ear, half-listening and then turned away, leaving just the memory of an arc upon the retina. If there was a word, I didn't hear it.

The trees stripe the sky like a barcode or a ladder of uneven rungs, stretching horizontally across the land. The road sends up spray. Hawthorn and blackthorn bushes are coming into blossom; the crows are building their untidy nests. If I had been born into another idiom, I'd have had different words to reach for the kind of thing I am trying to say. Hisham Matar said that you are born in the language you write in. I think about writing, and about what I am doing here, and how it is an attempt to create continuity with a series of fragments. And isn't that just like trying to raise the dead?

If I'd been born into another idiom, I'd speak about these paintings in words that matched their strength and arresting simplicity. But finding that idiom would be like trying to knit a symphony out of twigs. The words I have to hand are the only tools I know how to use. The paintings are spare, yet full of detail, mystically uplifting and mentally cleansing.

In my coat pocket, I have a pendulum, sellotaped to a piece of wood from your workshop floor, to prevent the balance spring from breaking. Depending on the weather in the house, when I get home, I will attempt to get this clock on the wall and the pendulum attached. The weather, emotional and physical, remains unknown, prone to squalls and lulls and bouts of puckery. I had to go to the coast to pick up the clock, which is an RAF sector clock, famous for its part in winning World War II. It is marked with five-minute red, yellow and blue triangles. It looks like it has been devised in the circus, used to mesmerise the enemy into giving away state secrets.

Just for fun, what did you dream of last night? My dreams are full of missing passages. Bottled messages rise on the tide, and are sucked back under. On the wall, there is a steady ticking, reminding me of history and time and all of the things we hoped we might never need to know. Caspian dreamed you had given him some money – a few hundred pounds – enough, you told him, to make a difference, not so much that it would prevent him from doing something.

Clan tobacco and a black cat called Lemon, because she smells like one; the brilliance of things normally never seen: the inside of a paint-tube; a skinned knee before it begins to bleed; wild hazelnuts in the August hedgerows. All these things were part of your gift, or perhaps your teaching, although your teaching could be sterner, more demanding. Twenty years of a tree's life burns in twenty minutes on the fire. We were children with scuffed knuckles and rough cheeks, sent out to play because play was what everyone should aspire to. The wind blew the doors shut behind us and there was nothing frivolous about it. In the barn, iron filings moved across the magnetic paper to spell magical signs and wonders; this is the right way to hold a chisel, an engraving awl, an aisuki – which is a Japanese cutting tool. When depression hit, you fell straight through the doldrums and into a place that made the sound of a heart hitting a tin roof. It was terrifying and we could not ignore it.

What is moss? It is a very ancient non-flowering plant, without roots, that stabilises whatever ground it is growing on. We made a collection: star mosses, pincushion mosses, fern mosses, sheet moss, fire moss. The questions we ask direct what we know, what we will pay attention to, how we will recognise what is necessary. What is art? It is a very ancient way of making marks that connect with what it means to be human. Art rescues us from fires and droughts. It is the medium through which we can retrieve what it was we were trying to say, but couldn't. We made a collection: Rothko, Caravaggio, Frida Kahlo, Tapies, Kandinsky. What we see directs what we will become, how we will live in the world, how we will live forever.

The geography of belonging, feldspar, limestone, millstone grit. These words carry a certain energy for me, conjuring up a deep, old space. It is a geography that dreams only of being itself. Silsden, rising out of the industrial north, hemmed by the Leeds and Liverpool canal with its whiff of wet stone, engine oil, castaway iron. I return there from time to time, wondering what I will find, and it is like returning to a dream. The streets are granular, the playground sunken. The clouds seem to be always glutted with withheld rain, waiting to fall and wash the windows of the back-to-back houses. I think of them as a string of lives, seamed in tragedy and tenderness, conducted in a language almost lost to me now, as blunt as a cow's head landing on the abattoir floor.

The hardcore years: bitter winters of chilblains and wet clothes. Rages indoors and out. Don't eat the snowberries – they are poisonous. We walked to school in the dark. In the dark, we walked home. We crossed the road because of fears of monsters in a certain house, although the monster was really at home. Summers of laburnums; don't eat the yellow blossoms – they are poisonous. Long days of dust and grass. There were rooms in the house that were artificially darkened. You would not talk to any of us. You curled up in the coldest room and chilled it further with misery. The cat was hit by a car and I brought her to you, her face hanging off. You took her into your hands, and we could not look at each other, for the terror of her torn face, but you did come out of the room.

When you were in the studios, we were not permitted to disturb you. Nothing was more important than painting. One summer evening, the cows came into the garden, massive as boulders from Ilkley Moor. They moved like underwater beasts, shouldering through gloom, swaying their bulk into the shadows, twitching under their haloes of flies. They churned the lawn on the shaded side of the house. Sepia roses collapsed under their hooves. Their flanks were the cracked black of wartime blackout blinds. Their breath misted the air. It was incomprehensible that they could be so huge and that there could be so many of them. Other days, there were peacocks on the lawn, spreading their tails, remonstrating. Sometimes I would lie in the middle of the grass and wonder what manner of beast it would take to prise you from the work.

At night I thought the sound of the wind was angels, placing their great feet, their mighty wings against the roof of the house, wolf angels blowing our house down. By day, I turned my back on them. The doors swelled with rain and had to be brayed into opening and closing. The cats curled up by the gas fire, snugged in. When it rained, the smell of oil paint and turps took on a different quality: heavier, more uneasy, like a church organ wheezing into tune. Those were the days of the huge dark paintings, six feet high, also angelic. When you emerged from the studio, it was as if you had scoured out your mortality. Though if it had gone badly, which it often did, you ticked with an unwatchable temper.

There came a time when small acts of rebellion were what kept you going: hoarding empty tins, wearing your funeral suit to garden in, going out to lift the long shadows from the grass. Even then there was something rangy about you – unpredictable, volatile – though it had softened into something so removed from rage it was as if all that belonged to a different era, a time when even the food we ate would be unrecognisable today: peppered tripe, haslet, cockles, semolina. If we entered a room without warning, the blackout blinds rattled, brittle enough to trap a bird in them – a little wagtail maybe, bewildered at finding itself out of sorts in a house it cannot recognise. I saw one today and it made me think of you.

Some rooms remain with me: the green room at The Gables, the darkroom above Amulet, the lean-to kitchen at King's Head. I remember the herbs falling in burning bunches, charred as dead birds in a forest; I remember the smell of chemicals in a tray as we developed film; I remember the light falling on the Victorian marble fireplace and how cold it was as I learned to recognise the words for all the different colours. There were other rooms in these houses, of course, the mangle in the washroom, the Independent Order of Rechabites Salford Unity poster in the indoor toilet. Before sleep, these days, when I lie down in my body, I allow myself entry into each one of these rooms again – silently – as though they are utterly empty of memory.

Robin Hood's Bay. Below the cliff face on the cold, damp sand that never sees the sun, we are gathering gull feathers, hagstones, holed shells. We are looking for Whitby jet. Little sand flies hop out of invisible holes. Seaweed – carrageen and bladderwrack – pops under my gritty feet. We have walked down from Ravenscar, our hunched backs holding up a grey cloud. Under there, you told me as we walked, lies Robin Hood's Bay, where the smugglers brought in French lace, brandy and tobacco in the 1700s. We might find pirate's gold. Better than that, we might find fool's gold, iron pyrites. I couldn't work out the homonym, and it didn't matter. We were treasure hunting. High on the crag, someone lit a bonfire, and the sparks flew up into the air, as exciting as anything we might find in the dark.

Portrush and a day of crossings between one life and another, moments when the world came loose from itself and tilted me. Gulls and crows swarming the vast sky. Sunlight; Flashes of rain sluicing the promenade. Black rocks; headlands; the devil's washtub; Arcadia; sands in shadow and sea bouncing back the light – so bright it hurts to look at it. Still dazzled, I caught the inkling of a soul behind a car windscreen. I had to look twice, and it bolted straight through me. I know I must have looked as though I'd seen a ghost. It was like that, but more real, and something detonated inside me.

The day gathers itself for another storm; something shivers in me at the deep atomic levels of the body. The trees ruffle the grey sky. A crucible of starfish empties from the clouds. No-one can tell if this is fabled or real. Something is crooked. Twigs catch in the seaweed, the harbour walls silver and then tarnish. The storm is undeflectable, a twist in the air, as singular and bitter as vitamins. Circles upon circles upon circles which is the way God intended it. Rain falling sideways into everything. Hope falling vertically into the white breakers to crash against the rocks. The rocks make their own art, on the cusp of skill and accident. I wait for the noise, but when it happens, it happens far out at sea. In all the wind and rain, you lean in and blow words into my head: forget about sorrow, let's crank up the joy.

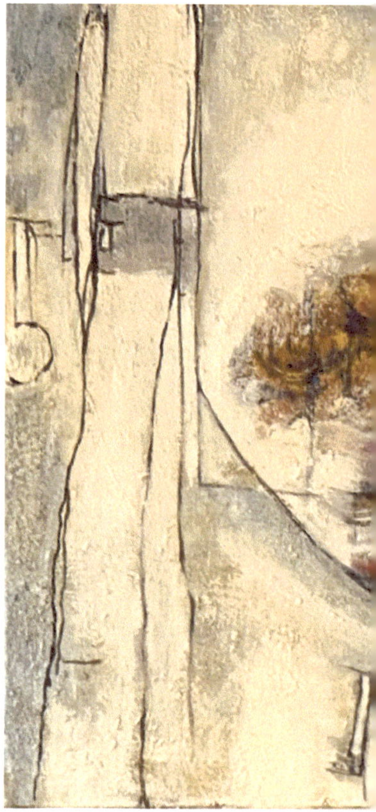

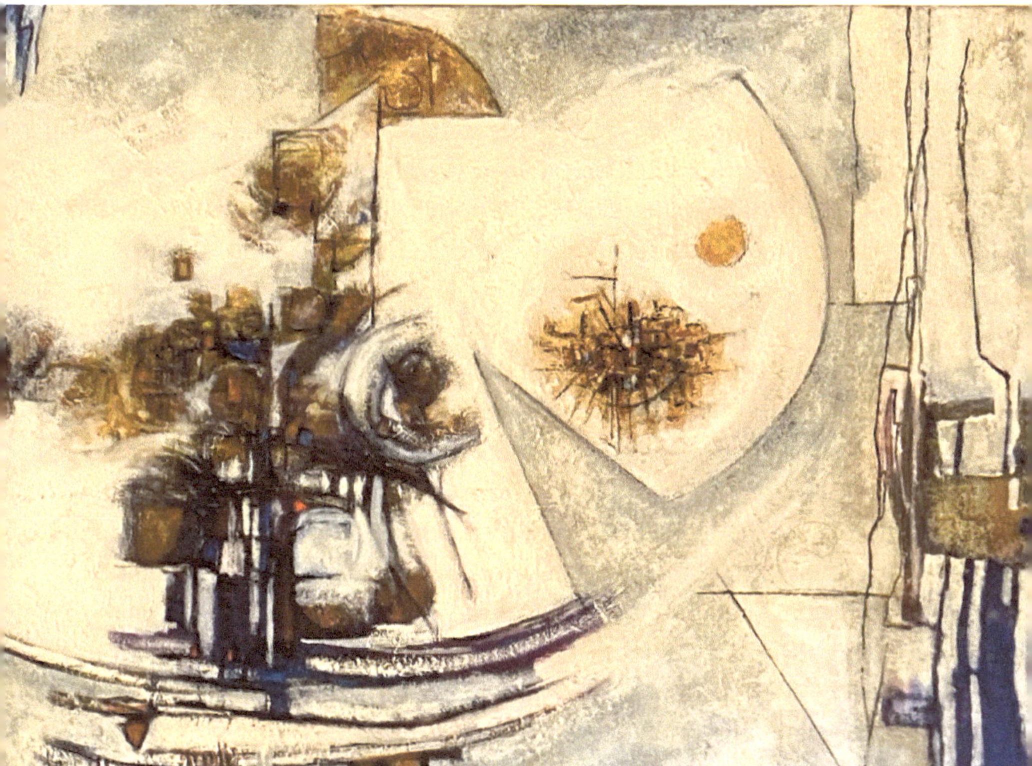

If proof were needed, this is proof. There is no art that can spare us the separation of death. The angels might look down from their shelves of cloud, but ultimately the studio lies empty, the smells of turps and oil lift themselves so high they might be simply ghosts of smells. I move around in it, and feel the weight of my own body in the space where thought has stopped. Even memory is recidivist, in that it keeps happening, or else it keeps forgetting. I find it hard to tell the difference. When it comes to these unfinished works, I look at them and wonder what it is you would have done next, how you would have resolved this one or this. The thing I keep coming back to is that this is not a resting place.

Of course, the work is halted mid-thought. Your mind blew wide open. I imagine it now as a sort of plunge towards clarity, although it expressed itself as confusion. But that's just for mortals. For months you seemed close to vanishing, but not in the way that you actually did. The candour of that still unsettles me. I heard that someone has turned over your grave, that it has fresh earth upon it. There's a sort of anguish to that news. To distract myself, I wonder if, like the soil, you are subsiding, falling into wrack and ruin, composing new shades, new forms that come right from the body itself. Perhaps, underneath all this, you are conjuring out of yourself the makings of a relic. Remembering how you hated to be disturbed when working, I hope with all my heart that you were not disturbed.

I can hear a dog howling, tethered to an outhouse out on the moor. Or perhaps it is the wind. I can hear the damp blooming under the wallpaper, or a kind of salty residue rising through the limewash. I can hear the fire going out, logs falling into ash, little embers flying upwards. I fancy I can hear the wine forming a residue crust in the glass, the unknown past sagging in suitcases of old photographs. If I lie very still, I can hear rain being passed from leaf to leaf in the woods at the end of the garden. I can hear all these things but you are a silent film of yourself, clapping your hands, laughing. You are beyond recall. I cannot hear a single thing, just my heart beating in my ears.

What is art? It is the ability to slow the body down or to step out of life for long periods at a time – long enough to see things differently, to hear something no-one has heard before – but which will be instantly recognisable as absolute. It resides in the quality of the doing, unravelling a sense of what is known to reach the sense of what is unknown. It is both a relinquishment and a replenishment. It is a way of making room for error and redeeming it, so it is both godly and human. It is a form of meekness and a form of mightiness. And every so often, it encourages us to see the funny side.

Your tree, the silver birch, marked out by the moon, shines then shivers as a cloud passes over it. Who knows what the darkness discovers? The night is chock-full of it. I dip my fingers into burnt umber and fingerpaint across old photographs. It obliterates parts of their story and releases something new, a layer of my self, smudged over unknown lives. Your tree loosens a small branch, a twig, a handle for a hand-made mark-maker. I gather these things to work with, as surely as clues, trying to discover what they remind me of.

The more I look, the more I see. In this landscape, which is so much more than a dreamscape, a man lies under the rusting disc of a sun. Sparks flint off the walls and land in shifting planes of earthtones. This is very tender. Though that might be a fluke, a consequence of my mood rather than yours. Was it winter, late afternoon, your brushes loaded with light, you fighting to get the last of it? If I look closely, I see the far hills outlined in soiled gold. Or is that absurd? A travesty of what it was really like? Sometimes, when I spend time like this with a painting, I am in a quandary between the matter-of-fact and the transcendent. Nevertheless, the more I look, the more I see that something fine continues to exist.

There's a strange concentration that marks dementia. A kind of focus that comes from the act of gathering. You were in way over your head. But each thing you turned over revealed itself as something new, and in that newness a delight. I think about all the waterfalls we have lived by: those in Silsden and Hawes; the little gushing falls that burst from the hillside at Stalling Busk. Now you are buried against Aysgarth Falls. What goes over the weir is swept away to the mighty ocean. The ocean will make its own heavy weather of it. Or not. Smuts of soot in the rain change the colour of the day. Harlequin lifts a dainty foot and sets off across the unmappable distance between here and the weir.

Again and again, unanswered silence. If silence can be heard above the high whine of tinnitus. There are gifts for those who learn patience. The moon tonight is a crescent of rose gold foil, a wishing moon; it rose in time to hear the last of the day's birdsong. If I am attentive enough, there is a sense of someone at my back, though I know better than to turn and look. It is a felt sense, a not-quite-breath, just a steady presence. All around me, the garden is inking itself in for the night, trees getting larger, more saturated. Lights go on. Someone opens a bottle.

In the garden of my childhood, by the dark-leaved bush, you are smoking. The blue smoke mingles with the cold air, and the smell of summer stocks. When I draw close, you tell me it's the thing you like best about smoking, the smell of tobacco on the air.

I breathed it in and I thought I could see what you meant. It was like a lilac dust had settled on the garden. It is strange, in retrospect, why memory chooses this one moment to recall, this scrap of conversation to snag in the mind's *wunderkammer.* These things come to me in scraps and fragments, like a puzzle it might be possible to solve.

There must have been many days when you reached for a word and couldn't find it, and that small loss seemed entirely normal. It wasn't, to begin with, a matter of erosion so much as distraction. The honeycomb mind had not yet started to disintegrate. Or perhaps it had. When it did, the effect was the exact opposite of the plenitude of a word. Holes were punched into the pages of memory to make a new kind of text of it. I remember you telling me that the more you focus on a single word – its etymology, its kinship, the journeys it has taken to arrive where it is, always on its way somewhere else – the richer and deeper its meanings become. But dementia brought a thinning to those depths. Words became so thin they were transparent and then invisible. Nevertheless, there were whole lines of poetry etched into your brain, and they could always be called upon, even if their meaning was on its way to being something else.

Here's a painting: assured, graceful; its lines both serendipitous and achieved. Its colours straight from nature: ochre, grey, gold. Its forms subtle, lucent, mantled. It is a rough square, bifurcated by a single, continuous line. It might well have been a painting, and one you would have enjoyed solving the problems of – how to get this line to represent both a fissure and a connection; how to make the two parts cohere and yet remain discrete – but it is not a painting, or not yet. It is a broken flagstone, full of texture and occlusions, perfectly cracked in two by weather's art. I enjoyed it just as much as a painting, and I also found a broken hinge that was, if possible, even more beautiful.

The fettler sifts through the contents of an old tin: here are screws, washers, files of different sizes, feathers; seedheads, old coins. They take on purpose as he looks at them. They would be nothing without him, without selection. It makes me think of how memory rests among objects and bestows upon them a particular light. This old tin of treasures suggests endless experimentation, and also abandonment. A fragment of broken wing mirror, a fleeting smile, a whetstone. When I look at these things, I make a bet with myself on what will rise and be chosen, and what will succumb. I'm wrong, of course. They all succumb. But, soon, I am sure that something among them will rise.

The dale is full of alchemy: the deep tin lakes that reflect the sky back to itself; the sun as it sends out its last line of gold rope to lasso the horizon; the caprice of evening when the skylarks let loose their last song of the day, a clarion call to night. Real things, lots of beautiful real things, happen more than once. Cows ruminate in the fields, switching flies. Or perhaps they cogitate. Who is to say which is the more noble of the two verbs? Cow parsley embroiders the edge of the woods, stitching its strange perfumes to the cold air. Politely, we return indoors; no need to say anything more. Everything we feel is shared: a brick in the chest, too large to ignore. The best we can do for it is to turn it into an ingot and make it shine.

The world was your elegant sufficiency, and your delight in it, and gratitude for it, remarkable. I see that now. You moved through it at a deep level, attentive to its myths, its histories, its poetries. I saw things in your paintings before I could see them in the landscape. The distinct zigzag of the road between Bainbridge and Stalling Busk: the way a field might be seen in the layers of its service to man; the way a rocky overhang becomes more than itself in the dark. Each thing, you tell me, resists comparison. Each thing is entirely itself, full of its own absolute information.

Your paintings abound with images of the chalice: arcs balanced on the lip of the land. I am struck by how intimate that relationship is. What is the purpose of a vessel? It has to separate the light on the inside of it from the light on the outside. Maybe the vessel is a house: a place we enter and it changes us. Maybe the vessel is a holy cup: a receptacle for what will be the miracle of transubstantiation. A vessel has to cohere. A crucible, a pot, a kettle, a copper bowl, a jug. Maybe it tilts so that what is happening in there, dips to the rim, is almost somewhere else. The purpose of the vessel is to enable restless thoughts to settle and be contained. The purpose of the vessel is stillness.

I was thinking about the sense of self, and how it is constantly being revised: updated, reinvented, rebooted. I was thinking about how we accommodate things that we would rather not accommodate, and how we might – with a strenuous act of will – walk away from them. How there are no continuity police who say that you have to carry this memory forward with you from yesterday until today. So far, so commonplace. But how does this fit with dementia? How did you manage those revisions when what remained was a whiteout. How did you make such whiteness seem true? These are questions that I can barely ask, let alone answer. But as we walked the hills again, I know that every tree saluted you, every nodding harebell bent its head. And I know that, like you, in that very way, I want to remain myself right up until the last minute.

Stainless, a small blade discovered in the dust; stainless as in unmarked by rain and weather. It was stamped into the earth, like a bone, or a piece of shale. In the old woodshed, a paper hive, large as a moon, thin as a seed of honesty; a few lazy bees still moving around it. The particular scent of oil on the hinges of the door. The smell of the shed, the cobwebby light. How would you achieve these colours? The colour of the stainless blade: phthalo blue, yellow, Payne's grey, cadmium white. The colour of the hive: white on white, burnt umber, let down with trimmer. Do you mean thinners? No, trimmer, a slake of something to shorten that white down to something that is almost not a colour. Isn't it interesting that to trim means both to cut something down, and to embellish it?

Blossom, drifting in the darkness (like thoughts), snagging on hedges, ledging in gutters, needing only the weather to make it disappear forever. Night falls, quick as warm rain. On my desk is the chalice you made from copper, verdigrised like a seascape, foam lifting and falling. It sits so true and strong. It is unmoved by grander things, but calls my attention back to it. Copper, mined from the earth, then weathered, heated and hammered, was the first metal used by man. It does not rust, is easier to work than stone. The moon shifts and something coppery on the air rings out of the dark. Blossom, falling from the ceanothus in tiny spores, like oxides, porphyries, bluets, snagging on memories, settling in the heart, or the lungs, shortening the breath.

Something is lodged in my chest which feels like a bone. Sometimes, when people are displaced, they lift the bones of their ancestors and carry them with them when they leave. What remains when presence goes? What remains of us in the land we once belonged to? Is it the thought of presence, the notion of a recaptured moment when we might return to each other, a scent on the air – vanishing? The wind meets itself coming back, coming in from the east and the north. Everything blows the wrong way. We walk towards the fate we know will happen, but we refuse it in any case, even after the event. It is as though I cannot bear the world without you in it. I am bewildered by the idea – cast into a wilderness of the unknown and unhoped for.

But life is surely experienced as something true, even if its elements seem strange or unrecognisable. As you moved through the months that were lit – or shadowed – by dementia, things no doubt loomed large and also, somehow, familiar: an outcrop of millstone grit with sphagnum moss catching the last of the light; the way a road bifurcates the landscape; dandelion seedheads moving through the soft air, breezing through time. All these things strung between being and nothingness, like ideas before they are formed, like new paint in unopened tubes. Behind us, a cat moves through the shadows, barely visible. It is both cat in general, and cat in particular; it is both cat historical – all the cats we have ever loved – and cat present – the one dear to us now, who is about to enter the house and settle into her purr. The cat's identity is both these things and neither. We should call her Schrödinger.

The chalice, sometimes represented by a simple arc, symbolising transformation, religious freedom, the feminine principle, appears in so many of your paintings. In the 15th century Andrei Rublev painted the icon *The Trinity*, considered the most famous of all Russian icons. It depicts three angels sitting at a table on which is a chalice containing a calf's head. The three angels gaze into eternity, each looking in a different direction. You knew the chalice was out of proportion; you could see it shouldn't work. You held up your thumb to obliterate it. The strength of the painting dissolved. Or rather, it unresolved itself. The chalice is the fundament of the painting, foreshadowing the eucharist, the centre around which the angels gather. From time to time, I hold up my thumb to mask out a chalice in your paintings, to see again where the foundation is, that place around which any holy conversation might take place. From time to time, I cover the chalice tattooed on my inside wrist to still myself, and listen for the thing that will bring me back to the silent contemplation of my foundations.

I've got it all wrong. When I stand by your grave, I am sure that the Falls are down and to the right, but it can't be. The Falls are behind us on the left. So, what is the roaring to the right of you? I cross the gates, follow the steep slope down, past the abandoned mill, through the copse of trees. I mark the yellow leaves, the catkins, the rush. Now the water is to my right. If I let it, the sound will drown out all the other sounds. If I let it, I can almost believe that this is the sound that I can hear as I stand by your grave, which, let's see, must be across those fields and up. Unmistakable.

I recovered a file, much rusted and with no edge to it, from a puddle behind a skip. The story opens with a rasp, something shaved away, some smooth unseen thing coming into view. The grate of metal against surface. A grazed knuckle where things did not go well.

If I seemed quiet, it was because of what I was thinking. What happens to thought when the words go? You begin with a brush, or something that makes a mark, a line on the canvas. It doesn't have to be a brush. It doesn't have to be a canvas. You begin with a thing that makes a mark, and then you make a decision. First the mark (let's say a line in the dirt), then the decision (let's say, intersect it). Without these two things, nothing can exist; not a tilled field, not a wall, not masonry, not portraiture, not the idea of the artist as a man. A line in the dirt, a blade to scrape it back, just a glint of what might be.

The shambolic days bunch up under the sky structures of light and wind and rain. The bench is wet with foxgloves, aquilegia, buckets of roses. A mirror behind the pansies bedazzles the light. Mint grows wild among the wallflowers. The ceanothus is a blue parasol for the bees. Children are blowing fairy liquid bubbles into the air. When I came indoors, I went straight to one of your paintings to look at it again. In the top right-hand corner, a sun, or a shape I take to be a sun, raised in sharp sand; green underpainting, pink or maybe apricot or umber on top, casting its light over the rest of the painting. I remember being told that in a child's drawing, the sun always represents the father. Is this the God's-eye view? A charm, an amulet. If I allow my gaze to wander, there you are again, deep in one of the painting's tunnels, all light gone.

Suggestion: just molten glass, a haze in a kiln, then – in the cold air – watch as everything moves from fluent gold through fire into ember and finally ash. It's incendiary, mystery made solid. Just smoke and the curl of incense in the air. You turned upon the freshness of that, smack bang into something glorious. Flux, rain on a mirror, just a bit, and then the blacksmith's alchemy. A paralysed ripple in the metal: reticulated. The temptation is to make everything beyond redress, like the sound of someone talking in a nearby room: indistinct yet compelling. And it is like that, for a micro-moment, before the thing itself and the picture of itself coalesce and become one hardened brilliant version of the idea. Then the content is made clear and everything that seemed hazardous, emotional, volatile, settles. At the end of the day, it is as sweet and complex as a spoonful of homemade raspberry jam on a spoon of Russian silver. Behind this door is the way we used to live.

Behind this door are foxgloves in a copper pitcher of water, swallowing the summer evening down their mottled throats. Hope comes in on the breeze, stirring the old, screen-printed curtains with their residual smell of oil. The light is doubled, tripled, quadrupled into a green continuum, flowing. Someone far below is watering the geraniums. Behind this door are stories told and retold as the light drifts, fades, swells, lifts and finally drops. Great happiness also settles amongst us for the evening. Wine is poured; if we are not joyful now, we will be soon.

What else is there to say? Maybe something about what it feels like to take a loaded brush to the canvas when life feels very constrained; what it feels like to paint a crooked line. Heart racing, chest aching, drawing close to the sacredness of things. Which mark came first and how do you know when something is finished? What sweet spot do you have to arrive in that says here, now, in the world: this is inevitable and unique? When I look at the works they seem complete, but I could not tell you where they began, which was the original line that led to this line that led to existence.

I know the studio by the smell of paint on torn cloths, of Windolene, of industry. I know it by the clean north light that pours in. I know it by the shelves, on which: small skeletons, pencils, home-made compasses, driftwood, masks, books, notes to self, stones, copper, stuff. The air keeps still in here. It remains the same, even long after you have no longer moved it around. The sun set across the dale in great folds of pink and gold, so vast and gorgeous that to look at it did not describe its impact. It was as if, standing there, I was part of the sunset, disappearing into it. It was me and I was it. And sometimes, if the light and the smell and the sound of the day is right, it is the same thing when I look at a painting. It is everything, and there is nothing that is not it.

Mask: The colours vibrate against each other. Nothing is steady. Or is that my gaze degrading? Sometimes when I look at this painting I see the rain-glazed bronze of Rombald's impassive stare, towering over the landscapes of our childhood. Sometimes I see my own face. Perhaps we think bronze and stone are less suffering than man, but it would be a category error. They are incomparable. Nevertheless, the giant of the north withstands the wind and rain and drunken high spirits, just as we must. He withholds the crushing blow, but still the threat is there. Like his, the lavish scaffolds we construct to make a self, will scab and flake and erode beneath the endless obligations of days and nights. Like his, our arms ache with all that we cannot let go. The slate roofs of Keighley are briefly caught in veils of silver, and then they darken. Is that my shadow disappearing down the street? What was it that you said about ghosts not having shadows?

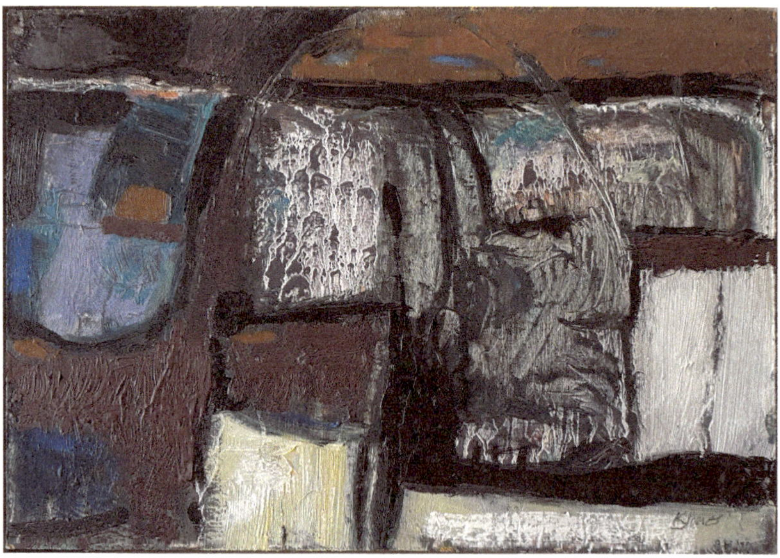

The gale that blows in from the land stings his eyes, causes the romance of his face to ridge. Coal dust dampens his lungs. A dab of water spots his forehead. Under ochre, the tenderness of lilac, the shock ping-ponging in the heart. A grimy sun sinks below the chalice of the horizon. Beyond this, a miner tending his allotment, harvesting his hoard of potatoes. Beyond this, a cacophony of crows in the high trees. They say the weather will break. Something snags – joy perhaps, or grief. He paints the mask to face a garden shut in by rain. He turns again to the restorative chemistry of burnt umber, white sulphur, phthalo blue, turmeric.

This painting among others, a lullaby dredged from memory. The smell of resin, oil, wood, rust. Punch on location, hill country in rainy weather, all other sounds subdued by the hoarseness of the storm. Six miles there and back. You find the best you can; stay alive. The hillside all around you, like a glow in a dark pool. Shadows flexing and bounding on the abstract of the moor. Treasures include sheep's wool washed dirty by the rain; the broken blade of a knife to score a line. A clock chimes, time's nemesis; the sound of breaking plates; the sound of the furnace lid being slammed shut on our wooden toys; passionate, terrible rages. And then silence, like the silence that lodges between stones. As well as this, a bin full of brushes. As well as this, a tin full of turps.

Light filters through the shadows, trailing its glitter of mica and dust. The world is slowly disintegrating around us: disassembling itself into particles. They will lay upon every surface and then they will be disturbed. Someone will traipse through the studio, grab a brush or a cloth, wipe through thought, wipe through reflection, forming and unforming dimensionality. There is surely some grace in this. Together we fall under the spell of the earth's restlessness, gathering its random treasures, a coin of battered silver, a twist of sheep's wool, the anonymous signature in the dirt. Dust to dust to gold. Something glitters at the edge of sight. Something that came from a time before this time. If I can make my mind wide enough, I will recognise it for sure.

In the spirals there are the windings of an inner life made visible, and not just an inner life but an ancestral life. Here are the references to the coal mines: dark earth descending, withholding itself in the dark, revealing itself in the dark, coils and coals, seams of time rendered to the human eye. There is gold there, too. And other minerals, signalled by blues and oranges and greens. The markings of a slow, interior formation. Earthly alchemy. Men bend their backs to the stone roof of the earth, scored with lines and symbols; each mark the making of a rough creation, revelatory, incandescent.

Morning. Birdsong tumbles out of the branches. There are fresh flowers on your grave, a bit early for Father's Day, in a tin can from your studio. Bees shake in the replicas of their shadows as they nose into the foxgloves. I dreamed of you, for the first time. Or perhaps I recognised you for the first time in a dream. I wanted a word from you, but you just smiled and disappeared, as though you had nothing on your mind, as though the consequence of things was no longer material to you. You are, in practical ways now, rooted in the real world.

Father's Day 2023: the year rolls around again. It's a strange perspective, getting to the edge of things. All year I have been gathering all the small nothings and trying to bring them into some sort of being. But then the world is mostly full of invisible things. And the work of art is to bring those things into our vision, to hang them in the gallery between one moment and the next so that time is immaterial and what moves us is not urgency or nostalgia but immanence.

The thing I recall when you draw close, is how solid you were. How safe you made me feel.

Acknowledgements

The writing of any book is both solitary and a collaborative project, and there are many people without whose support and care for detail this book could not have been written. For all the varied communities of writers and friends who have graced my home and my workplaces with their insights, humour, beauty and spontaneous discoveries, I am deeply grateful. We worked in wonder, always just one layer away from glory.

Immense thanks are owed to Jill Glenn, who was both long-suffering and generous in her editing. This book would not have been nearly so fine without her stringent interventions, and getting it into print would not have been anywhere near as much fun without the shared laughter and vision. Thank you, Jill. I doubt the book would have existed at all without your belief in me or your encouragement of me as a writer.

My family has been the greatest blessing of my life: together you have formed the crucible that has fired me to be who I am and write what I want. Thank you all.

Finally, and posthumously, thank you to my parents, who brought me up to believe that to be creative was the highest calling in life – there could have been no finer maxim to live by. It has rescued me again and again.

Constellations Press is a small independent press,
committed to publishing works of fiction, memoir and essays.
We publish books that boldly reimagine society and
celebrate our diverse humanity, adding to the
total sum of the world's beauty.

constellationspress.co.uk

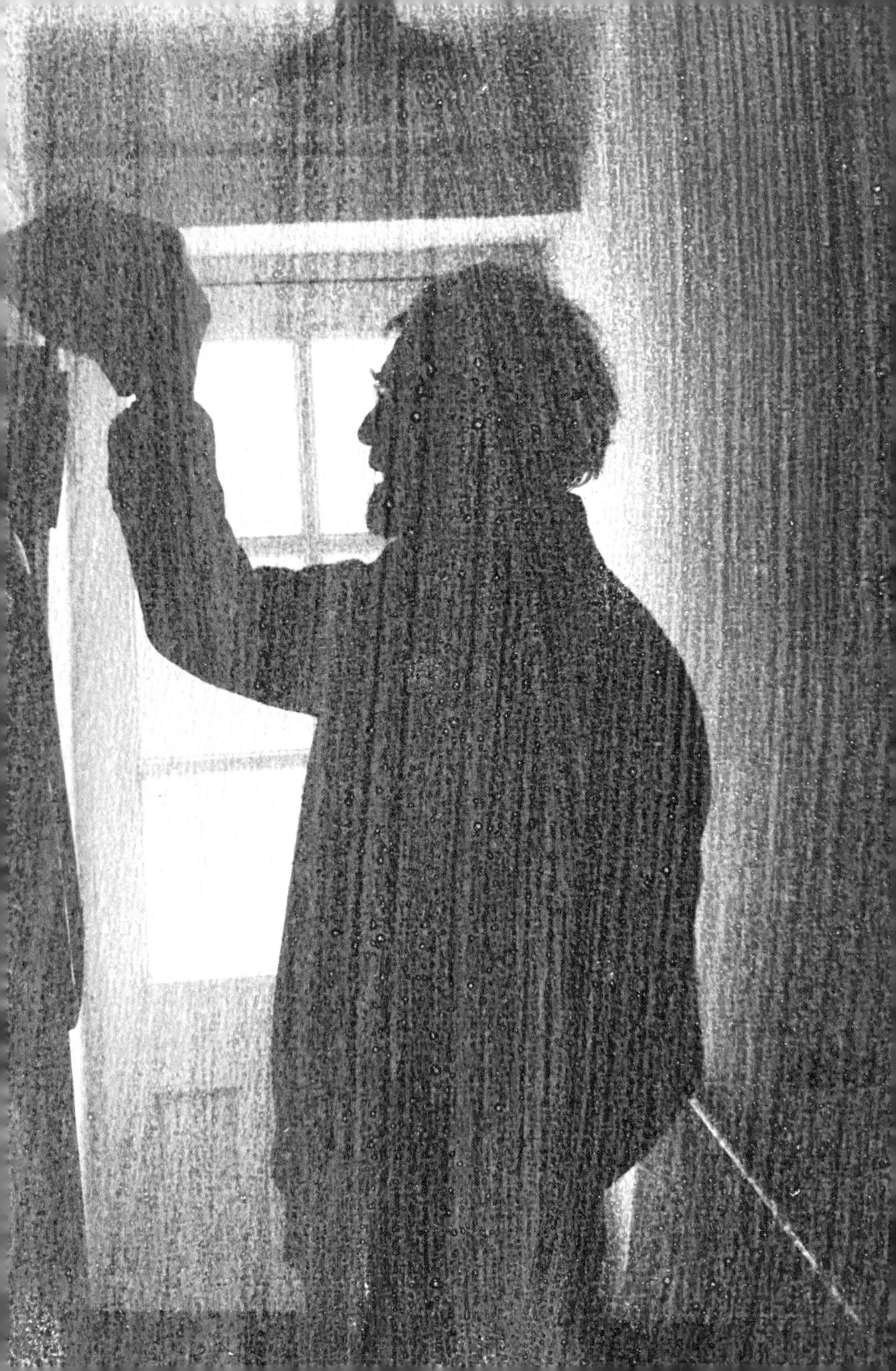